"Stay Away from Me, Luke."

"The whole time we've been talking, I've been loving you in my mind."

"Stop it," she ordered softly.

"I'm half-crazy, wondering if you still taste sweeter than candy, whether you—"

"Luke—"

"Still put perfume between your breasts."

Resenting the fact that he still possessed the power to arouse her, she folded her arms across her chest and whirled away from him.

"It's no use, darling." He stood behind her and gripped her shoulders, fitting his lean torso to her soft curves. "You can't hide from love."

Bonnie knew she had to nip this in the bud, before the fire in her veins blazed completely out of control. . . .

CATHLYN McCOY

is a free-lance writer and romance novelist who says she spends every spare moment at her typewriter. Her other favourite activities? Playing the guitar, bowling and visiting Alaska—she loves those long nights!

Dear Reader,

Thank you so much for all the letters I have received praising our SILHOUETTE DESIRE series. All your comments have proved invaluable to us, as we strive to publish the best in contemporary romance.

DESIREs feature all of the elements you like to see in a romance, plus a more sensual, provocative story. So if you want to experience all the excitement, passion and joy of falling in love, then SILHOUETTE DESIRE is for you.

I hope you enjoy this book and all the wonderful stories to come from SILHOUETTE DESIRE. If you have any thoughts you'd like to share with us on SILHOUETTE DESIRE, then please write to me at the address below:

Jane Nicholls
Silhouette Books
PO Box 177
Dunton Green
Sevenoaks
Kent
TN13 2YE

CATHLYN McCOY

On Love's Own Terms

Silhouette *Desire*

Published by Silhouette Books

Copyright © 1984 by Cathlyn McCoy

First printing 1984

British Library C.I.P.

McCoy, Cathlyn
　On love's own terms.—(Silhouette desire)
　I. Title
　813'.54[F]　　　PS3563.A266/

　ISBN 0 340 36167 0

Printed and bound in Great Britain for
Hodder and Stoughton Paperbacks, a
division of Hodder and Stoughton Ltd.,
Mill Road, Dunton Green, Sevenoaks,
Kent (Editorial Office: 47 Bedford
Square, London, WC1 3DP) by
Richard Clay (The Chaucer Press) Ltd.,
Bungay, Suffolk

On Love's Own Terms

1

Odd that a wedding should reunite them. Her younger sister and his little brother . . . who'd have ever dreamed Luke and she would wind up shirttail relatives?

Bonnie Ford clenched her hands into tight fists and shoved them into the pockets of her white cotton chinos as she stamped across the meadow. She didn't *want* to feel this way—torn between family loyalty and her own anxieties about seeing her ex-husband after seven years. For her sister's sake she was trying to divide past from present, to separate bitter from sweet and share the nuptial excitement with a smile.

But it wasn't easy. Since Bonnie's arrival from New York last night, her sister had lionized Luke as if he were a candidate for sainthood and Santa Claus combined:

"Luke had a Waterford chandelier shipped from Ireland for our new house in Atlanta. Wait til you see it! And he promised he'd be our first dinner guest, too, once we're settled.

"Luke says I'm the best thing that ever happened to his family. He always wanted a sister, you know.

"Luke insisted we use his vacation home in the Bahamas for our honeymoon. While we're away, he's going to install a sunken marble tub in our bathroom.

"Luke just called from the gas station on the highway. He'll be here *any minute!*"

It was that last statement which had driven Bonnie out of the house. She hadn't excused herself or explained her rude reaction to *Saint* Luke's impending arrival. She'd simply escaped through the nearest exit.

Macaroni spine! Bonnie berated herself, fully aware that she was merely postponing the inevitable.

Her sister had decided to hold the wedding in their childhood home, forty miles northwest of Atlanta. With both sets of parents deceased, Bonnie and Luke were doing double duty—standing as maid of honor and best man during their younger siblings' ceremony, then co-hosting the small reception afterwards.

Triple damn! Didn't anyone back in that hectic marriage mill realize how awkward she felt about spending an entire week in his company? Especially after the horrible way they'd parted!

A chill trickled along her spine, and she tipped her face to the sun, seeking its warmth as she walked in yesterday's shadows. She'd vowed to work civilly with Luke, and she would, for her sister's sake. No one ever need know that the pain of their marriage still tormented her soul.

At the far edge of the meadow where she and Luke had laughed and played as children, Bonnie paused and drew a deep breath. Tiger lilies and doily-shaped Queen Anne's lace had overgrown their old baseball diamond. The waterfall over west had whittled a steeper slope into their favorite sliding rock, but the pool at ride's end still looked icy. From what she'd seen of it so far, Rebel's Ridge hadn't changed all that much since she'd fled it seven years ago.

But she had. The change was more than physical, though she'd certainly fulfilled the promise of beauty that had been hers as an adolescent. Bonnie's wide amber eyes reflected compassion as readily as they sparkled with amusement, because she'd seen her share of sorrow. A generous smile remedied her slightly crooked front teeth; a Limoges complexion made one overlook the few stubborn freckles sprinkled across the bridge of her slender nose. Her hair had deepened in color to spun autumn honey and was cut to softly frame her face. Lithe and leggy, she collected clothes and wore them with the flair befitting a successful New York City caterer.

While her southern drawl was less pronounced these days, Bonnie's voice retained a slow-molasses warmth which charmed her numerous clients and utterly frustrated her dates when she bid them a friendly but firm good night at the front door.

Luke had introduced her to love; his rejection, coupled with her body's own betrayal, had shattered her sense of self-worth as a woman. Since their divorce, she'd built a prosperous business from scratch but she'd avoided emotional investments with a once-burned determination that bordered on obsessive.

"Bonnie!" Her sister stood on the back porch, calling her home.

Luke was probably waiting there now to discuss the remaining details that needed attention before Saturday. Her stomach fluttered, and she knew she wasn't ready to face him just yet. Besides, she'd certainly done her fair share of waiting around for him during their pretense of a marriage.

Let him sit and stew awhile, she decided, turning instinctively to climb the wooded hill where she and Luke had loved away that incredibly innocent spring before their elopement. Inside the tree-shaded circle, Bonnie leaned against a hickory trunk and felt the bark scraping her back as it had when they'd first embraced. Like an old friend who hasn't forgotten, the peach-blossom breeze sighed a welcome.

"Bonnie!" Her sister's voice reached her ears easily, but she ignored it and closed her eyes, recapturing those stolen moments of her youth.

Luke Ford had been her idol long before he'd become her lover. Five years older than she, he'd spent endless summer hours improving her batting stance, instructing her in the sneaky art of the spitball, stealing her heart even as he'd taught her to steal second base. It was Luke who'd shown her how to noodle catfish along the banks of Tucker's Creek; who'd helped her through algebra; who'd sampled her mudpies, then later eaten every bite of her burnt mistakes when she was first learning to cook.

During her senior year in high school, their relationship took a dramatic turn. When his father died, Luke dropped out of college a semester before graduation and hired on at the nearby marble quarry. Bonnie had been the first to recognize how much he hated the dead-end labor, how disappointed he was that he hadn't found work in the construction field. He hadn't complained; she'd simply sensed it.

Because Luke's salary went toward helping his mother and little brother, and because he was too proud to let Bonnie finance their weekend fun from her allowance, dating became a test of their young and healthy imaginations.

In January and February, rather than attending the picture show in town, they had roasted popcorn in her parents' fireplace and watched old movies on television. Hamburgers on the grill in March and April had tasted much better than anything served at the local drive-in. Warm weather had enticed them outdoors for leisurely walks in the woods behind Bonnie's house, for home-packed picnics in what had become their circle.

It happened as naturally as rivers flow downstream, as gently as the meadowlark's fluting lullabye. Having carried a man's load all winter, Luke needed a woman. Having adored him all her life, Bonnie found a remarkable satisfaction in learning his loving ways. She knew for certain that she was pregnant a week before she turned eighteen, and they eloped the morning after her birthday.

"Bonnie!" Her sister's voice held an urgency that escaped her, because she was trapped in another time.

She'd lost the baby early into her fourth month; he lost his job the following month when the quarry declared bankruptcy. From there, it was a downhill slide to divorce court.

Depressed about her miscarriage, bored with "playing

house," Bonnie spent all her time in the kitchen testing new recipes and preparing elaborate meals that her meat-and-potatoes man refused to eat. Unable to find another job, Luke stopped coming home at the end of the day and began hanging out until all hours with his similarly unemployed buddies.

Their arguments escalated in both frequency and volume; even their bedroom became a battleground. One night, she had followed him to the local bar and caught him dancing with a flaming redhead who'd wrapped herself around him like a sweet potato vine. Cut to the quick, Bonnie had yanked off the ring Luke had slipped on her finger in a preacher's study, flung the plain gold band in his surprised face, then driven straight to her parents' house.

He had not contested the divorce or appeared in court. And Bonnie had been left to mourn the loss of their baby and the death of their marriage, blaming herself for both as if it were her due. A week after the judge dissolved their vows, Bonnie received a check in the mail for half their meager mutual property. She'd promptly cashed it and caught the first northbound bus. Luke's tomboy had cried a woman's tears all the way to New York City, the farthest she could run and still afford the cooking classes which would launch her career.

The leaves rustled in his wake as Luke stepped out of her past from the heavy hickory limbs and bending pine boughs shading the circle they'd once considered sacred.

"Who says you can't come home again?" he quipped. "Pigeons do it all the time."

For a split second, Bonnie was tempted to run once more. She didn't *want* to see him again! But renewing her resolve to get through this week as graciously as possible, she opened her eyes and looked directly at him. "Hello, Luke."

He was every inch the man she'd foreseen in her first and only lover. Crinkles fanned from the corners of his brown eyes toward his temples. Time had darkened the wind-blown hair framing his roughly cut features. His chest was wider, his shoulders broader, yet his masculine physique was as taut and lean as ever. Overall, maturity fit him as neatly as the faded jeans defining his long, muscular legs.

"Darlene and Dave were about ready to turn the bloodhounds loose on your trail." That lopsided grin, so endearing in the boy, was dazzling in the man. "I told them I had a hunch I could find you."

Bonnie stiffened defensively. It was foolish to feel caught, but she did. Her escape plan had backfired. Or had it? By climbing the hill rather than heading home, hadn't she practically invited Luke to follow?

Too flustered to reason it out right now, she averted her head to hide her confusion and shrugged indifferently. "I took a walk, thinking you might appreciate a few minutes alone with the kids."

"Hell, they're not interested in anything but each other these days." His understanding laugh flowed as richly and warmly as buttered rum. "Outside of 'Hi, Luke; Bonnie went out the back door,' they hardly noticed me."

"I know what you mean." Smiling indulgently, she dared a glance in his direction. Maybe she'd worried unnecessarily about this meeting. "I've felt a bit like excess baggage myself since I arrived."

He took a cigarette and a monogrammed gold lighter from the pocket of his chambray shirt. "I'm sure the only reason that Darlene started hollering for you to come home was so I'd quit taking Dave's attention away from her."

Their friendly remarks paved the way for a congenial discussion about the wedding. Amazed by their affability after the bitterness that had marred their marriage, Bonnie relaxed somewhat as they talked. In a short period of time, they'd efficiently divided the remaining duties, settling the question of who was in charge of what.

"Enough about Dave and Darlene," Luke decreed, leaning against the tree trunk opposite her as if he intended to stay for a while. "Tell me about Bonnie."

She tensed again. With their present alliance still so tenuous, it hardly made sense to rehash those awful days and lonely nights she'd spent restructuring her life. *Keep it light,* she decided, forcing a smile that didn't feel the least bit natural. "There isn't much to tell, frankly. It's your typical small-town-girl-makes-good kind of story— grade-B movie material all the way."

"I've probably got most of it memorized," he admitted. "Darlene corners anybody who'll stand still long enough to listen while she brags about her big sister." He chuckled. "If I didn't know better, I'd swear she was part magpie."

"Thanks a bunch!" Bonnie faked a huffy tone. "For your information, buster, she sounds like a broken record when she talks about you."

"How so?" he prompted.

She smiled, this time genuinely. "Every week or ten days she seems compelled to call—collect, mind you—and regale me with the details of each new project your construction firm has landed."

"Remind me to give her a raise," he drawled, "retroactive to her first bout of boasting."

"What about my phone bills?" she teased.

With a sudden, disturbing intensity his gaze raked from her stylish leather sandals, over her chic silk tunic, to her neat, fashionably cut hair. "I'm sure you can afford an occasional telephone call."

Unnerved by his cynical observation, Bonnie realized they'd lingered long enough. The fact that she could obviously provide for herself was probably an insult to his manhood, especially in light of the way they'd struggled to make ends meet before their divorce. She glanced at her slim gold watch, dropping a subtle hint.

"We whipped some pretty improbable odds for a pair of poor 'crackers,' didn't we?" he challenged curtly.

"I suppose so." Standing proudly, she returned his regard. She'd botched marriage and motherhood. Damned if she'd apologize for making a go of her career! "Luke and Bonnie, the proverbial long shots, hit pay dirt."

He laughed mirthlessly. "The good life," he mocked. "It sure beats the stuffing out of that shanty-town existence we led back when, doesn't it?"

"I suppose so," she repeated softly, disheartened to hear him describe their marriage in such derogatory terms. How he must have hated her then! Tears stung her amber eyes, and she blinked to keep them at bay. Was he deliberately trying to spoil the fresh start they'd made today? Or were they both bedeviled by some of the same old ghosts?

It struck Bonnie in a jolting burst of clarity that she had returned to their loving circle on purpose, hoping to begin releasing her hold on yesterday. But rather than making peace with the past, as she'd planned, she found herself reliving it.

Luke dropped his cigarette and crushed it under the toe of his boot. Fascinated by the rippling interplay of his muscles, Bonnie fought the treachery of her emotions and lost. Lord, she'd almost forgotten what a genuinely big man he was! Her heart hammered in alarm as she recognized the purely physical nature of her response, but logic proved a poor match for passion. Apprehension shimmied through her while she wrestled with her own desires more fiercely than she'd ever battled with her ex-husband.

He must have sensed her turmoil, silent though it was. Luke looked up, his dark gaze scanning her delicately troubled features as he, too, seemed to wage a private war with himself.

How long they stood there, not speaking yet visually devouring each other, Bonnie couldn't say. She only knew that the tension mounted so fast, it crackled like a live wire dropped in water.

"We'd better head back to the house," he suggested tersely. His mouth slanted in a thin smile. "Otherwise, Darlene and Dave will think we've lost our way."

Vaguely disappointed and very confused, Bonnie nodded. She'd survived the skirmish, but the victory felt inexplicably hollow. She turned to leave, then paused beneath a pine bough and glanced back at him.

"I haven't thanked you yet for helping Darlene."

"It was nothing." He dismissed her gratitude with a shrug.

"Well, I worried terribly about her after mama died, but she was dating Dave and refused to come live with me." A faint note of sadness marbled her voice. It hurt to admit her younger sister had found the happiness that had eluded her. She cleared her throat. "When you hired her as office manager for your construction company, it took a real load off my mind."

"I like Darlene." Luke's husky tone wrapped Bonnie in a velvet chain of memories she desperately wanted to forget. "She reminds me of a girl I used to know."

A dizzying sense of déjà vu enveloped them, and Bonnie's eyes flared wide as she faced what she'd feared most about coming home. They had grown up and fashioned successful professional lives from the ashes of their personal failure. But neither time nor distance had dulled this need for one another. If anything, absence had only intensified it.

"Do you feel it?" he demanded abruptly.

"Yes." But it was a reluctant admission.

Luke came toward her, bridging the careful gap they'd kept between them.

Bonnie hesitated, torn between instinct and indecision. It would be so easy to meet him halfway and mold herself to his hard male contours. And so easy to repeat their tragic mistakes. She stood her ground. "Stay away from me, Luke."

For all it accomplished, she might just as well have whistled into the wind. There was little haste but plenty of purpose in his stride as he closed the distance between them.

"The whole time we've been talking, I've been loving you in my mind."

"Stop it," she ordered softly.

"I'm half-crazy, wondering if you still taste sweeter than candy, whether you—"

"Luke—"

"Still put perfume between your breasts."

His gaze slid suggestively to the front of her blouse. As though he'd touched them, as if they remembered the feathery caress of his fingertips, her nipples tightened and strained against the silk fabric. Resenting the fact that he still possessed the power to arouse her, she folded her arms across her chest and whirled away from him.

"It's no use, darling." He stood behind her and gripped her shoulders, fitting his lean torso to her soft curves. "You can't hide from love."

"Love?" The pain of his betrayal quivered in her voice. "You wouldn't recognize love if it sprouted wings and flew into your face!"

"Call it what you will—"

"It's defined as *lust* in my dictionary!"

The heat of him warmed the whole length of her. Luke pressed his cheek against her hair while his strong hands deftly massaged the stiffness from her shoulders. Bonnie knew she had to stop this now, before the fire in her veins blazed completely out of control.

"You want me as much as I want you," he whispered.

"No," she protested.

As his hands glided down her arms, his mouth explored the sloping hollow where her neck met her shoulders. "I feel it in the way you're trembling, Bonnie."

She spun around, catching him off-guard. Flattening her palms against his solid chest, she pushed him backwards. He'd left her no choice—she had to hurt him. It was strictly a matter of self-preservation.

"Don't flatter yourself," she snapped. "Haven't you ever heard the expression, trembling with rage? Just remembering why I divorced you, that's exactly what I'm doing."

His dark gaze drifted to the front of her blouse again, taking in the hardened tips of her breasts.

The more he hated her, the safer she was—she simply couldn't afford another emotional risk. Bonnie let him have it with a deliberate cruelty that sickened her.

"And don't attach any great importance to my physical reaction," she warned. "I still crave corn pone on occasion, too, but I'm certainly not interested in a steady diet of it."

Luke's glare confirmed she'd hit her target, but Bonnie took no pride in her accuracy.

"If you think you sound sophisticated, think again," he advised. "Leading a man on, then disappointing him, is nothing but a juvenile trick."

"You came on to me!" she reminded hotly.

"You weren't fighting me off."

She winced at the truth in his words. "I was confused," she admitted. "For a minute, I . . ." How could she tell him she was hurting, too? She couldn't. "I've learned some hard lessons in seven years, Luke—the most important one being the difference between love and lust. If you—"

"Considering that that wasn't love we felt just a minute ago, it wasn't a bad substitute," he said caustically.

Even knowing she deserved his sarcasm, she was hurt by the remark. "You haven't changed a bit! All you want is an instant replay of the past: Luke scores and Bonnie pays the penalty."

"Spoken like a true martyr," he scorned. "If I recall correctly, we shared the satisfaction as equally as we did the suffering."

"You'd better see a doctor," she retorted, "because your memory seems to be fading real fast."

Bonnie reeled away from him again, her throat constricting painfully as she was harshly reminded of the baby she'd lost. Deep inside, she had never stopped blaming herself, wondering what she'd done to cause the miscarriage. She drew a bracing breath of air even as the tears spilled freely down her cheeks.

"All I remember is that when I needed my husband's support the most, he was busy drowning his sorrows in a beer mug and dancing his sadness away in a damned roadhouse."

"If you'd been more of a wife—"

"Says the model husband?"

The silence thickened with other accusations that didn't bear repeating.

"I'm sorry, Bonnie." Luke's voice was filled with regret. "I know it's probably too late, but believe me when I say I never meant to hurt you."

She nodded, wordlessly accepting the apology she'd

never dreamed she'd hear. Bonnie turned around and was shocked by the bitterness she saw in his dark eyes. Ashamed of her part in provoking the fight, she wiped her eyes with the back of her hand. "I'm sorry, too."

"If I'd known then what I know now, I wouldn't have let it happen." Luke looked so miserable, it wrenched her heart. "I was older; I could have controlled things if I'd tried."

"It wasn't *all* your fault," she qualified with a watery smile. "I could have said no, if I'd wanted to."

"Listen, I don't want to spoil the wedding," he said. "If my hanging around all week means you'll be uncomfortable, I'll head back to Atlanta and stay put until Saturday." He lifted an eyebrow, leaving the final decision to her. "Hell, I see Darlene and Dave every day; this is your first visit in years. Say the word and I'll disappear."

How could she deny him the pleasure of helping prepare for the ceremony that he was partially financing? With a bemused expression, she shook her head. "You're not worming your way out of shelling walnuts for the wedding cake *that* easily."

His smile would have charmed the stripes off a skunk.

"Why don't we declare a truce?" she proposed. "We won't talk about the past—that'll be off-limits. And the wedding folderol should keep us too busy to fight."

"Agreed." Luke proffered his hand, then promptly withdrew it. "Before we shake, though, I have to ask one question on the forbidden subject."

She eyed him warily, then nodded.

"For the reception, are you baking that fantastic chocolate cake I used to love so much?"

"Yes; it's Darlene's favorite."

"Are the walnuts I'm supposed to shell going into that creamy fudge frosting you were always asking me to help you stir?"

"That's *two* questions." Bonnie was stymied by his sudden interest in what she planned to serve. They'd already agreed that the food for the reception was her responsibility.

"Humor me," he urged with that effective lopsided grin and an innocent shrug of those wide shoulders. "I'm getting to the point as quickly as I can."

"Yes." She sighed and tapped her foot impatiently. "The walnuts are going into the fudge frosting."

The wicked gleam in his eyes should have warned her. Without touching her, Luke leaned over and placed his mouth a whisper away from her ear, as if the trees could hear. "Remember what we used to do with the extra fudge?"

His question bolted through her like white lightning. After their first erotic episode with the sweet, creamy chocolate, she'd made a habit of stirring up a batch-and-a-half every time. Just in case. Bonnie refused him the satisfaction of a verbal answer, but her scarlet cheeks confirmed that she did, indeed, remember.

"Cease fire!" he proclaimed. Luke grabbed her hand and pumped it, then draped his arm around her shoulders. "Come on," he encouraged with a friendly squeeze, "I'll walk you home."

She shot him an appraising amber glance. "Go on without me," she insisted. "I'll be along in a bit."

"Hey, are you all right?" His embrace tightened slightly.

"I'm fine," she asserted in a falsely cheerful voice.

"This is my last chance for a little peace and quiet before the wedding, and I intend to take advantage of it."

In truth, she needed the solitude to sort through the newly tangled mess of her emotions. She waited, thinking he'd take the hint. When he didn't, she shrugged out of his brotherly embrace.

"Scoot!" she ordered. "Before I forget I'm a lady and give you a shove."

"I'm going. I'm going." Luke raised his hands in mock fear and did a ludicrous reverse goosestep. Just before he ducked under the pine boughs and disappeared, he veered dangerously close to violating their recent treaty. "If you do forget you're a lady, I'll be more than happy to remind you." He winked. "Curing amnesia is my specialty."

"I'll just bet," she replied skeptically.

When she was certain he'd gone, Bonnie released an exhausted sigh. The next week stretched ahead of her like a long, wearying journey down the same old road. There had always been an element of the extreme in their relationship—love or hate, laughter or tears, hugging or hurting. It was probably downright foolish of her to believe they could straddle the middle line, even for a few days.

Her glance strayed around their circle. Things hadn't changed as much as she'd hoped—he was virile; she was vulnerable. If that wasn't a recipe for trouble, she'd trade her wooden spoons and copper pans for a wedge of humble pie.

2

ᴏᴏᴏᴏᴏᴏᴏᴏᴏᴏᴏᴏ

Their truce lasted until dinnertime.

"Bonnie, you know I never eat anything that floats," Luke grumbled as he glared into the soup bowl she'd passed him across the table.

Dave cleared his throat and shifted uneasily in his chair when she set his serving in front of him. Peering curiously into the bowl, he asked, "What do you call them?"

"Ping-Pong balls," Luke sniped.

"Quenelles," Bonnie corrected calmly as she ladled soup from the porcelain tureen. Ignoring Luke, she directed her explanation to Darlene and Dave. "They're similar to dumplings, only they're made from meat instead of flour. I used chicken for these."

"Delicious!" Darlene pronounced after biting into one.

Following his intended's example, Dave took a cautious nibble, then smiled. "Different," he declared, "but real good."

The three of them started on the first course of the delectable meal, which Bonnie had spent the afternoon preparing. She had made the dinner as a celebration of their family reunion and had added a silent plea for peace.

Luke saw to it that her prayers went unanswered. He sat opposite her, his soup untouched, paying undivided attention to her mouth. Now and then a crooked smile lifted the corners of his own mouth, as if he found something amusing in the way she ate soup. Bonnie knew she wasn't dribbling. But every time he grinned, she automatically raised her linen napkin and dabbed her lips and chin. It couldn't hurt to be on the safe side.

He's doing it deliberately! By the time she realized what he was up to, her hand shook with the effort of lifting her spoon without spilling the soup. She lowered her gaze, studying the interior of her bowl as if it were a crystal ball. Why was he baiting her? Worse yet, why was she rising to it? The clear broth held no answers, only a solitary quenelle.

She counted to ten, impatience surging through her veins. Unaware of the tension at the table, Darlene and Dave chatted happily. Damned if she'd let him ruin her dinner! Her cheeks flaming an angry scarlet, Bonnie looked up and licked her lips with the tip of her tongue. Luke's eyes shot such electric sparks that she went hot and cold all at once, every cell in her body tingling with excitement.

Forcing herself to break the magnetic connection,

Bonnie stood and turned toward the kitchen. Round one belonged to Luke.

"Darlene, would you clear away the bowls while I bring in the meat and vegetables?" It was a perfectly normal request, yet her voice sounded strange—quite unlike her own. Bonnie walked the interminable distance from the table to the swinging doors, acutely aware of Luke's potent gaze following her every move.

The kitchen was familiar turf. While she mentally regrouped, her hands functioned automatically. She arranged stuffed lamb chops on the meat platter, poured a velvety hollandaise sauce over the steamed asparagus and unmolded the wild rice ring.

"Why didn't you fix the steaks I brought from Atlanta?" Luke greeted her with the loaded question when she wheeled the carved walnut serving cart into the dining room.

"I'd already planned the menu for this evening," she explained patiently. She flashed him a tight smile, betraying none of the fury she felt. "We'll have the steaks tomorrow night," she reasoned. "Okay?"

Bonnie managed to fill four plates and pass three with a deceptive domestic tranquility that left her bursting with pride.

Round two looked rather promising, she thought. But her complacency proved completely premature.

Ignoring his food, Luke repeated his visual attack. His dark eyes narrowed suggestively whenever her fork disappeared into her mouth; his grin widened devilishly whenever she lowered her eyes from the aggressive challenge in his The juicy lamb chops, the tender asparagus, the fluffy rice—they might well have been sawdust for all she tasted them.

Still oblivious to their older siblings' silent combat, Darlene and Dave ate heartily and talked nonstop about their wedding and the house they were building in Atlanta. Bonnie nodded and smiled every time it seemed appropriate that she do so, but the conversation could have been conducted in gibberish as far as she was concerned.

It was a battle-weary Bonnie who finally abandoned the pretense of eating. Mumbling a lame excuse about having sampled too much as she cooked, she laid her fork aside. Although her hand itched to slap away the triumphant smile on Luke's face, she squelched the urge and stood.

"I'll go plug in the coffee maker," she announced brightly to no one in particular. "When you're finished eating, leave the dishes for later. I'll meet you in the living room with the coffee tray."

The kitchen was a warm and friendly haven. Through the years, hundreds of relatives and neighbors had gathered around the old formica table, gossiping, laughing and swapping recipes and tall tales. Why then, out of those untold numbers, was the memory of Luke the only one that came to her mind while she worked?

Bonnie took cups from the cabinet, spooned sugar into a bowl and filled the cream pitcher—routine actions that required no real concentration on her part. How many midnights had Luke and she raided this old refrigerator? She ran her hand along its smooth porcelain surface, recalling in unappetizing detail some of the weird ingredients they'd slapped between two slices of bread and called a sandwich. How many evenings had Luke and she sat up over her algebra papers, redoing each problem until she understood what to do with the x's and y's well enough to earn a passing grade?

Those moments and others swirled around her now, dancing like dust motes in a stream of sunshine. After their marriage, she and Luke had stood in the middle of this kitchen, hands tightly clasped, while announcing their elopement and her pregnancy to her parents. Later, she'd sat alone here, sobbing out the hurt, sorting out the uncertain future.

Methodically, Bonnie finished preparing the coffee tray and carried it into the living room. Dave sat in the overstuffed recliner, paging through a sports magazine. Darlene knelt in front of the entry-hall chest, rummaging for something in the bottom drawer. Luke stood staring out the bay window, his broad shoulders backlighted by the scarlet rays of a stunning sunset.

"Who wants coffee?" Bonnie set the silver tray on the low table in front of the sofa, then perched on a cushion to pour. Dave accepted a cup; Darlene said she'd fix her own in a few minutes.

Bonnie glanced up at Luke's unyielding silhouette. If only he'd cooperate! "Let's see," she began in an optimistic voice, "you drink yours black if I remember correctly."

He spun around, his stubborn expression exterminating her hopes for a halfway pleasant evening.

"I found them!" Darlene proclaimed with a laugh. Holding a small cardboard box, she fairly waltzed across the room and plopped down beside Bonnie. "It's your half of the family photographs. Mama divided them before she died and put yours away for safekeeping." She lifted the lid off the box. "Let's have a look at them."

Bonnie and Darlene browsed through the photographs, taking a sentimental visual journey through childhood and adolescence. Dave continued reading. Luke kept his distance.

"Lord love a duck!" Darlene hooted, closely inspecting one of the pictures. "Where did you get this steel-wool hairdo?"

"Don't you remember the hell I raised when mama gave me that home permanent and left the waving lotion on too long?" Although Bonnie could laugh about it now, it hadn't been a bit funny at the time. "I cried three days straight and refused to leave my room. Finally, to shut me up, daddy drove me to his barber and told him to keep cutting until the frizz was gone. The guy practically scalped me!"

"I loaned you my baseball cap," Luke recalled out of the blue, "and you wore it everywhere for a solid week."

Bonnie looked up at him, and their gazes locked. For a wonderful moment time reeled in reverse, erasing old sorrows and wrapping them in the sweet cocoon of youth. Darlene stood. Luke walked over and claimed her place on the sofa.

"When I took the cap off Danny Tyler called me a skinhead, and you punched him in the nose."

Luke chuckled. "The next day you brought me a batch of chocolate chip cookies you'd baked—all of them burned black as pitch on the bottom."

"You ate them."

"Every last crumb."

Unnoticed, Darlene and Dave left the living room.

"Will you just look at these?" Bonnie asked rhetorically. She scooped the entire pile from the box and set them on her lap. "Why, I'll bet you're in every other picture."

"Let's see." Luke slipped his arm around her shoulders and leaned closer.

Dusk fell as softly as a down comforter. Together, they examined the photographs and traded the souvenirs they had saved in their minds and hearts. Bonnie groaned occasionally in embarrassment. What a skinny creature she'd been—her legs looked just like matchsticks in this one! Luke's frequent laughter reverberated vibrantly in her ears. Whatever had happened to all those baseball trophies he'd won in school? Probably serving as doorstops all over town, thanks to his mother's famous rummage sales.

When they came to the pictures taken during their marriage, they both lapsed into silence. Here she'd mugged for the camera while he'd pointed at her bare feet with one hand and the small but definite bulge of her belly with the other. There, after her miscarriage and the quarry closing, Bonnie's eyes were deep pools of pain and Luke's grim expression seemed chiseled from stone. There'd been no reason for either of them to smile.

On the brink of tears, Bonnie gathered her composure while returning the photographs to the box and replacing the lid. "I'll take these upstairs and put them in a suitcase before I do the dishes."

Luke's arm remained around her shoulders.

Keenly conscious of the intimate press of their bodies, she groped for emotional distance. "I saw a beautiful leather album last week in New York. When I get back to the city I think I'll buy it. Sort of an early birthday present. To myself . . ."

Luke's hand slid to the nape of her neck where his thumb made lazy circles that felt like billion-volt brands. Bonnie trained her gaze straight ahead. If she looked at him, even for an instant, she was lost.

"Do you realize this is the first time we've ever slept under the same roof without sharing the same bed?" he murmured.

Stung by his question, she stood. "Only if you don't count the nights one of us slept on the sofa after an argument."

She started toward the stairway. The box she carried felt as heavy as lead; it was so full of memories. She'd sort them out later, behind closed doors.

"Wait!" Luke stood and came after her.

Of their own volition, her feet stopped walking. She stared down at them in amazement. *Traitors!*

"Look at me, Bonnie."

"No. You'll just make those come-to-bed eyes."

He took her arm and turned her around. His smile was incredibly tender. "Surely you can't fault me for noticing what a beautiful woman you've become?"

Her skin burned beneath his strong grip, and she jerked free of his hold. "Don't smooth-talk me, Luke."

"I'm not," he protested. "But seeing those pictures—"

"Made you wonder if Miss Roundheels might topple again?" she interrupted bitterly.

He shook his head, mutely denying her accusation.

Bonnie grasped the box with both hands and hugged it to her aching heart. "Seeing these pictures had an effect on me, too. They made me realize how much I disappointed my parents, and what a lousy example I set for my younger sister." It took a supreme act of will, but she faced him squarely. "They made me ashamed all over again of what we did to our families, to each other and to ourselves."

"Damn it, Bonnie, haven't you forgiven yourself yet?" Although Luke sounded grave, he didn't seem angry. And when he clasped her shoulders, his hands were much gentler than she felt she deserved. "I'll bet under that silk blouse, you're wearing a hair shirt with *failure* printed across the front."

She lowered her head, humbled at being so astutely exposed, and let him draw her into his arms. Only for a minute, she promised herself, leaning against his muscled chest. *Only until the pain eases,* she vowed, pressing her cheek to the warm hollow of his wide shoulder.

He comforted her like he would a child with a skinned knee rather than as a woman emotionally paralyzed by her past. His body absorbed her shudders; his shirt blotted her tears. The box she held bonded them together through her storm of grief. When she was all cried out, he released her.

Bonnie experienced a flash of regret as she stepped free of his embrace, a reaction she quickly quelled. She'd already revealed too much of her turmoil. Keeping her head lowered to avoid meeting those darkly perceptive eyes she murmured, "I owe you an apology."

"For what?" He sounded perplexed.

"For all those terrible things I said to you today."

"I deserved them," he admitted in a rueful voice.

"Partially, yes. But I spread on the spite with a trowel,

and that really was unfair." Swamped with guilt, she ran her fingernail beneath the rim of the box lid.

"Sometimes we have to take a hard look backwards before we can go forward." Luke cupped her chin, forcing her to face him. "Confronting the past is part of the healing process."

"But it hurts."

"I know."

"I'm afraid," she protested.

"I'm here," he promised.

Dare she trust him again? Bonnie closed her eyes and felt his warm breath fanning her skin.

Luke traced the curve of her lower lip with his thumb. "I won't rush you, even wanting you as much as I do."

She looked at him and knew he told the truth. It was her first glimpse of hope in seven years—and it scared her.

"It'll get worse before it gets better," he warned.

"Can you take it?" she challenged softly.

He smiled, slow and sweet. "Darling, the worst you've ever dished out is still the best I've ever had. I'll take it in double portions any day of the week."

She blinked, dangerously close to tears again. After all these years, she'd become reconciled to living with her regrets and hiding her true feelings. It was a stifling existence, but safe. If she failed—

"It's your decision." Luke bent and brushed her lips with his, then let her go. "Take the risk and rediscover the woman. Or settle for the safety of self-pity."

Floundering in a sudden rush of fear, Bonnie backed up one step. He expected too much of her! She started to tell him exactly that when the box she held began caving in at the middle. She was clutching it too tightly.

"Let me help you." He reached out to her.

She stumbled up another step, retreating.

"Damn." He swore softly, but his tone was more threatening than thunder. "I've accepted the past and learned to live with it. You can, too, if you'll only try."

She stopped, spellbound by his haunted, dark eyes. "Why, Luke?" she whispered. "Why?"

"Because I still care." His mouth slanted in a self-mocking smile. "Because even when I wake up with another woman in my bed, I wake up alone." His gaze narrowed with a determination she recognized all too well. "Because you took half of my soul when you left, and I want it back."

His honesty nearly proved her undoing. They'd always been able to communicate physically. Time hadn't changed that; but it had changed them. Could they really reach one another on a more mature level? Or was this another pipe dream, doomed to end in the same old nightmare?

"Think about it, Bonnie," he urged.

"I'll try, Luke." It was the most she could promise at this point. Turning, she started upstairs. "If Darlene needs me for anything, I'll be in my bedroom."

"Aren't you coming downstairs again tonight?" he asked.

"No; I'm exhausted." She took the steps at a weary pace.

"I'll tell Darlene to do the dishes, then," he volunteered.

Should she say it? Bonnie paused, her foot poised on a

riser. The temptation overwhelmed her, and she pivoted, smiling innocently. "Did you mean what you said earlier about wanting to help me?"

"Name it and you've got it," he answered earnestly.

"You do the dishes," she retorted. Bonnie spun and scampered up the stairs.

Luke's laughter followed her all the way.

Oddly enough, silence woke her. The quiet here was almost palpable, a welcome respite from the round-the-clock street racket she'd become accustomed to as a resident of New York City.

For a while, she lay motionless—renewing her acquaintance with the rural night and lulled by the bullfrog concert coming faintly from the creek bank. A blue-moon brilliance bathed the bedroom when Bonnie sat up and hugged her knees to her chest.

Was Luke sleeping downstairs? He was too long for the "chastity couch," as he'd always cursed it while courting her, so he'd probably made a pallet on the living room floor. She smiled, imagining him sprawled in slumber only twenty feet below, and wondered where he wandered in his dreams.

A pang of sadness struck deep into her heart. If she hadn't miscarried, their child would have favored Luke. She didn't know why she felt so certain about that; she just did. The boy Luke had been scampered through her mind, his dark eyes flashing mischievously even as he slowed his pace to let her catch up and run with him. Only hours ago, he'd worn that same devilish smile which had enchanted her as a child and challenged her as a woman.

Had Luke really grieved for their baby? Or had he been relieved to be released from the responsibilities of a shotgun marriage? Painful seconds ticked away as Bonnie sobbed silently. She didn't know the answer because they hadn't discussed it when she came home from the hospital.

She had gone through labor and delivered a baby she'd never held in her arms. For weeks afterwards she had cried, aching with a despondent sense of loss and guilt. If Luke had suffered, as he'd claimed this afternoon and again this evening, he hadn't shared his feelings with her. In the end, they'd been nothing more than intimate strangers.

So why did she still want him? Obviously they had a sexual chemistry that wouldn't quit. But was their desire rooted in nostalgia, or was it a tender new offshoot that would flourish later if nurtured now? Bonnie's sigh echoed her bewilderment. If she was even remotely capable of separating the emotional from the physical, she'd be holding Luke tonight instead of hugging her knees.

What exactly did he expect of her? Was he suggesting that she close shop and come home? Impossible! Her business was booked solid through June with graduations, weddings and museum openings. In addition, an established publishing house whose parties she catered had asked her to write a cookbook for their American food series.

Regardless of her personal feelings, she had to return to New York and fulfill her professional obligations. Surely when she explained the situation, Luke would understand. A poignant smile curved her lips. One thing was certain: If practice made perfect, her leaving ought to prove flawless this time.

Doubts darted through her mind. Luke said he still cared. But for how long? Forever? Or just until she made some major misstep? He said he felt incomplete without her. In truth, hadn't she been living only half a life without him?

Bonnie's throat felt cottony with fear, and tears blurred her vision. She had lots of questions, but so few answers. Maybe she and Luke would find a solution. She shivered. Maybe they wouldn't.

The first silky pink strands of dawn threaded the sky before Bonnie surrendered to her exhaustion again. But she didn't sleep well. Dreams of Luke wouldn't leave her alone.

3

Bonnie felt like a genuine slugabed when Darlene shook her awake later that morning. Since she could hardly confess to her marriage-minded sister that she was exhausted because she'd spent half the night thinking about her own divorce, she improvised a hasty excuse about jet lag catching up with her and hoped for the best.

"That's odd, considering you didn't even change time zones." Darlene wandered toward the dressing table where she began poking around in Bonnie's cosmetics case. "Maybe the real reason you're so tired is because you're breathing fresh air instead of industrial pollution. I've heard that the mountains have the same effect on people."

"Mmm," Bonnie mumbled, "my lungs collapsed for joy."

Darlene laughed. Judging from the familiar fragrance,

she was also spray-testing Bonnie's favorite perfume. "By the way, your friend Sueanne phoned a little while ago. She said she'd love to get together with you one day this week if you have the time."

Bonnie nodded and made a mental note to return the call later today. All through school, she and Sueanne had been closer than two peas in a pod—swapping clothes and sharing secrets, supporting each other through head colds and heartaches. Sadly enough, she had never captured that same quality of companionship with another woman. Not even with her sister.

When Darlene finished with the contents of the cosmetics case, she sat on the foot of the bed and conducted a one-woman gabfest. That Bonnie neither responded nor opened her eyes didn't seem to bother her in the least. She talked enough for the both of them.

Bonnie finally decided to rise but seriously doubted she'd shine again much before the turn of the century. In the bathroom, she splashed cold water on her face. It helped. She brushed her teeth and combed her hair. Better still. When she emerged, she felt considerably more alert than she'd thought possible.

Her lace-trimmed nightgown floated around her as she walked toward the dresser. She selected underwear from the top drawer, then took out a pair of claret-red cropped pants and a matching camisole top from the closet.

Darlene ambled over to the full-length mirror and stared glumly at her own attire, a T-shirt, denim cut-offs and sneakers. "If Dave saw the two of us together right now, he'd swear I'm the victim of severe gene mutation."

"Why?" Bonnie asked as she slipped into her clothes.

"Because I ooze about as much sex appeal as the

Bride of Frankenstein while you look like the flower of southern womanhood in full bloom," she grumbled. "Even *I* find it hard to believe we're related."

"But you're dressed for moving furniture," Bonnie pointed out. "You'd look kind of silly carting end tables around wearing a Scarlett O'Hara hoop skirt."

"Maybe so." Darlene sighed. "But if you weren't my sister, I'd be insanely jealous."

Bonnie recognized the symptoms of self-doubt, having suffered numerous episodes of the same malady since her divorce. Were their fragile egos simply a peculiar family trait? she wondered. Or was this a classic case of sibling rivalry finally surfacing after all these years?

Looking closely at Darlene, who'd become a woman during her absence and without her help, Bonnie felt a sharp pang of guilt. Letters and long-distance phone calls couldn't compensate for the lack of personal contact between them, but she prayed they'd have time this week to strengthen their blood ties. Perhaps they'd also forge the precious bond of friendship.

Bonnie reached into her closet and removed a voile sundress she'd bought specifically to wear during her visit. It would be a small beginning, but she had to start somewhere. She took the dress off the hanger and held it up for size against a delighted Darlene. Despite their slight physical differences, it seemed a near-perfect fit.

"Now when you get back this evening," she instructed in her best big-sister voice, "take a long bubble bath, then slip into this. It's guaranteed to set Dave's head spinning faster than a top."

"It's gorgeous," Darlene murmured, stroking the soft material. "And shoes, too!" she squealed when Bonnie produced high-heeled sandals of delicately woven leather. Twisting and turning in front of the mirror, she laughed. "I'll be so dolled-up, Dave won't even recognize me."

"The Bride of Frankenstein, indeed." Bonnie sniffed indignantly, repeating Darlene's earlier description of herself. "Nobody talks like that about *my* sister and gets away with it."

Darlene carefully draped the dress across the bed to avoid wrinkling it, then grimaced. "Compared to you, though, I'll still look as homespun as sackcloth."

Bonnie realized this was the turning point as far as establishing the future course of their relationship. If Darlene had resentments to air or questions to ask, now was the time. She waited quietly, letting her younger sister take the initiative.

Rejoining Bonnie in front of the mirror, Darlene smiled ruefully at her own reflection. "When I was growing up," she confided, "I wanted to be blond and leggy, just like you."

"Whatever for?" Startled by the revelation, Bonnie gaped at Darlene, who was an attractive brunette.

"I suppose because everyone was always making such a big fuss over you," Darlene admitted without a hint of rancor. "Let's face it, around here you were the original golden girl—the prettiest, the smartest in school—"

"The one who got *caught*," Bonnie added dryly, referring to her pregnancy.

"Oh, but you even did that with flair." Leftover envy tinged Darlene's sigh. "Of course, I was only fourteen at the time, too young to voice an opinion of consequence. But if anyone *had* bothered asking me, I'd have told them I thought your elopement was the most romantic event since—" She flung her arms wide for emphasis. "Since Romeo and Juliet!"

"Right elements, wrong tragedy." Despite her bantering tone, Bonnie was jolted to learn that Darlene had harbored so many mistaken notions.

She walked to the window and gazed outside. If she were really aiming for an honest understanding between them, she had to set the record straight. "In reality, the whole thing was more like a terrible practical joke that backfired on us."

"Because of your miscarriage?" Darlene prompted.

"Partially." Bonnie frowned and shrugged her shoulders expressively. "The day we eloped, I kept having these horrible attacks of morning sickness." She shuddered at the memory. "Plus, I cried all the way to the preacher's house and back again, confused and scared witless."

"I wish I'd known," Darlene murmured sympathetically. "But you always acted so confident about what you were doing; it just never occurred to me that you might feel the least bit afraid."

"Try petrified," Bonnie corrected. "Remember daddy's old adage, We grow too soon old and too late smart?"

Darlene nodded and sat down on the foot of the bed again.

"Well, that described Luke and me to a tee the day we eloped." Her eyes misted with tears she adamantly refused to shed. "He didn't know the first thing about how to be a husband. And outside of a flair for cooking, I certainly wasn't very qualified to become a wife." An ironic smile curved her lips. "Unfortunately, by the time we realized our shortcomings, we'd already involved an innocent third party."

"Did you ever consider your alternatives?"

"You mean abortion or adoption?" Bonnie drew a deep breath and shook her head. "Not seriously."

"How did Luke feel about it?"

"He never said. And I was too damned frightened of what his answer might be to ask." She dipped her head in remorse. Perhaps after hearing the truth of the tragedy, Darlene would know what a vital role communication played in building a strong marriage. "In essence, we were strangers caught in the same snare."

"Then your miscarriage was sort of a blessing in disguise," Darlene concluded. At Bonnie's horrified expression, she hastened to clarify. "I mean because it freed you both."

"Physically, yes; emotionally, no." In spite of her firm resolve to the contrary, Bonnie felt tears trickling down her cheeks. "I don't know how to explain it except to say that once I'd adjusted to the fact that I was pregnant, I wanted that baby with every breath in my body."

"I never realized that before," Darlene admitted sadly.

"That was my mistake, too," Bonnie insisted. "I assumed you were too young to understand."

"When you moved back home before your divorce, I would lie awake in my room at night listening to you cry." Darlene sniffled softly as she stood and hugged Bonnie. "I hated myself because I didn't know how best to help you. And after you went away, I figured I'd failed you when you needed me most. If only we'd talked . . ."

"I've always wondered if I might have unconsciously

done something wrong early in my pregnancy that caused me to lose the baby." Bonnie sobbed brokenly as she voiced her secret burden. "Maybe I neglected eating the right foods. Maybe I lifted a heavy piece of furniture. Maybe I didn't rest enough or—"

"Don't keep punishing yourself when it probably wasn't even your fault," Darlene pleaded. "Listen, not long ago I read an article by a doctor saying miscarriages happen often in first pregnancies—they're a natural screening process with no known treatment to prevent them. He also wrote that the emotional complications are generally much worse than the physical."

"I certainly confirm that theory." Bonnie sighed heavily.

"Luke did, too," Darlene added bluntly. "For a long time after you left, he acted like a crazy man. When he wasn't two-fisting his way around town, he was holed up in that little house you had rented. He seemed to be shutting out the world and everyone who cared. Even though he's dated other women since, he's never gotten over you."

Hearing his reaction described so vividly, Bonnie realized how selfish and immature she had been in assuming that the loss was hers alone. Her mind whirled with regrets. Could she ever make it up to him? Why hadn't they talked it out between them?

"This doctor's term for couples mourning a miscarriage was *the walking wounded,* because they tend to bottle up their grief and their feelings of failure rather than discuss them," Darlene continued. "It's an excellent article, full of new information. I'm sure the magazine is still around here somewhere if you want to read it."

Bonnie nodded and wiped her eyes with the tissue that Darlene had pressed into her hand. Relief at having shared part of her guilt for the first time ever mingled with the warm certainty that she'd gained a friend. She looked at her sister and couldn't contain the sudden, lighthearted spurt of laughter burbling in her throat. "Aren't we a pretty, pink-eyed pair?"

"Too bad teardrops aren't pennies. We'd have our pockets full." Darlene smiled in watery chagrin. "Dave says I've got a maudlin streak a mile wide. Much as I hate to admit it, he's right."

"You just tell him it's a time-honored family tradition," Bonnie ordered pertly. "Some clans have good teeth; the Sob Sisters have well-drained sinuses."

A honking horn interrupted their chat.

"I'd better scoot before Dave comes after me." Darlene hugged Bonnie once more for good measure. "He's anxious to get the furniture moved into Atlanta this week so we won't have that hanging over our heads after the honeymoon."

"Can I help?" Bonnie offered.

"Later, maybe." Darlene hurried across the room. "Today, we're just taking what the two of us can handle." She rolled her eyes in mock disgust. "His van is loaded to the gills! I only hope there's room inside for me."

"I'll stay here and make out my grocery list for the reception," Bonnie decided.

"Good idea," Darlene agreed as she opened the door.

"Wait!" Bonnie stopped her sister halfway into the hall and pointed to the dress draped across her bed. "I'll hang it in your room and put the shoes in your closet."

Darlene grinned impishly. "If Dave starts working too

hard this afternoon, I'll warn him to save some strength for tonight." Her expression grew serious. "Thank you, Bonnie. That talk means more to me than a thousand wedding presents."

A lump lodged in Bonnie's throat, so she acknowledged her sister's sentiment and her own gratitude with a radiant smile.

Two impatient blasts from Dave's horn sent Darlene scurrying out the door. After Bonnie placed the dress in her sister's room, she went downstairs. Eerie quiet greeted her, and she presumed that Luke had accompanied Dave and Darlene to Atlanta. If he'd stayed, maybe they could have had their long overdue talk and cleared the air about how her miscarriage had affected both of them.

The fresh-brewed aroma of coffee beckoned her into the kitchen. She poured herself a cup, then sat at the table with pen and paper. Since planning menus was her stock-in-trade, the chore went rather quickly.

Now what? She carried her cup to the sink and rinsed it. Last night's dishes were stacked haphazardly in the plastic drainer. Who'd washed them? There was a merry twinkle in her eyes as she put the dinnerware into the cabinets. But the notion that Luke was in immediate danger of getting dishpan hands was more amusing than plausible. She could count on one hand the number of times that he'd helped her in the kitchen during their marriage.

That done, Bonnie removed the rural directory from a drawer and dialed her friend Sueanne's telephone number. When she didn't get an answer after ten rings, she hung up the receiver. So much for that idea.

More from habit than hunger, she perused the contents of the refrigerator. Lifting the foil lids off several bowls, she wrinkled her nose. Darlene's leftovers resembled badly botched scientific experiments. But recalling how as a bride she'd resented comments on *her* housekeeping, Bonnie emptied out the worst of it and took a vow of silence. If anyone actually had the stomach to inquire about the missing food, she'd simply explain that she'd made room for the reception dishes and let it go at that.

Standing at the sink while the disposal finished gobbling the garbage, Bonnie gazed out the window. A long, lean shadow near the tool shed caught her eye, and her heart lurched wildly when Luke rounded the corner of the small outbuilding.

Stripped to the waist, he was a hard-muscled sight to behold. Broad shoulders and a rock-solid chest tapered into a flat stomach and narrowed hips. As he spread a dropcloth and then crouched to smooth it over the lush spring grass, sunbronzed skin rippled an enticing invitation to Bonnie's tingling fingertips.

He carried four unfinished ladder-backed chairs from the shed and set them on the dropcloth, working with an easy rhythm rare in a man his size. A woman's heat smoldered deep inside her. Luke had a knack for pacing that Bonnie remembered exquisitely well. Even sowing passion's first seeds, he had tempered youthful urgency with a tender skill belying his inexperience. He'd never hurried—always seeing to her satisfaction before taking his own.

Turning the chairs upside down, Luke carved grooves with a penknife into the base of each wooden leg.

Watching him, Bonnie felt a surge of emotion which ultimately clouded her eyes. He had made these chairs for the kids, using his unique talent to create a gift of love that would serve them well the rest of their days.

The clatter of the garbage disposal signaled it had finally emptied. She silenced it with a flick of the switch, turned off the tap water, then went out the back door and across the yard.

He saw her approaching and smiled. Much as a lover's fingers would, the breeze mussed his thick hair. She fought a madcap urge to run to him and rumple it properly. Their shadows entwined in the grass although they stood slightly apart when she stopped.

"Just what I need—an extra pair of hands," he greeted.

"Ask and you shall receive," she quipped.

Luke's glance boldly skimmed the swell of her breasts beneath the camisole. Bonnie flushed, knowing she'd left herself vulnerable for a cheap shot. To her relief, he didn't take it.

"I really could use your help." He nodded in the direction of the overturned chairs. "They weren't sitting square enough to suit me when I tried them out this morning. If you'd hold them steady while I shave a bit more off the back legs, it would save me having to put them into the vise again."

"Sure." She skirted the edge of the dropcloth, knelt and gripped the one he'd been whittling when she'd interrupted him. "I'm ready whenever you are."

They made quite a team. Bonnie stabilized the frames while Luke measured, marked and trimmed the legs. Constructed of hard maple with seats woven with white oak splits, the chairs were built to last a lifetime. They were sturdy, comfortable and beautiful, she pronounced after testing them for wobbles. His glowing eyes showed his pride and justifiably so.

It only seemed natural that she help him stain them, too. Luke scrounged around and located another brush. Bonnie borrowed the work shirt he'd hung on a nail, rolled up the sleeves and wore it as a smock. After tying his red bandana around her golden hair, she slipped out of her sandals and wiggled her bare toes in the grass. Looking at her get-up, he just grinned.

While they worked, they talked, recapturing the platonic friendship of their youth. Old identities receded in the heat of the afternoon sun and the warmth of conversation. They weren't former spouses; they were friends. As such, they shared the task as well as the satisfaction of seeing it through to the end.

The staining done, Bonnie returned his work shirt and bandana before retrieving her sandals. Luke put the brushes to soak in turpentine, then set the chairs inside the shed to dry. They headed into the house where she prepared a pitcher of iced tea and he began thawing the steaks he intended to cook for dinner. Fixing sandwiches no sane person would look at twice, much less eat, they devoured the double-decker monstrosities with vulgar speed.

Content beyond description, Bonnie poured each of them a second glass of tea and made a few additions to her grocery list. Luke sat and smoked a cigarette. The silence wasn't a bit awkward. Words weren't necessary.

Neither of them knew in the waning light of a wonderful day that the calm merely preceded another storm.

"I guess I'd better plan on spending tomorrow in Atlanta." Bonnie folded her list and propped it against the plastic napkin holder in the center of the table. "According to Darlene, the market here doesn't stock even half of what I need."

"I'll take you," Luke volunteered.

"I thought I'd just go in with the kids and do my shopping while—"

"There won't be room in Dave's van for you, because they're moving the dining room buffet," he said. "Anyway, I have to drop by my office and sign some bids we're submitting on future projects." He smiled in a most disarming way. "Unless you relish the idea of riding to town in a silverware drawer tomorrow morning, I'm your next best bet."

"Okay," she conceded, "but I want to see their new house."

"You will," he promised. "In fact, I should stop by there anyway and see how the construction crew is coming along with the finishing touches. I've been working them overtime so it will be ready for Darlene and Dave right after their honeymoon."

"Do you think they realize how lucky they are?"

"I doubt it."

"It's partially our fault if they don't," she remarked softly.

"I suppose." He seasoned his gruff admission with a smile.

Bonnie stared into space, her mind's eye focused on the bungalow where she'd lived with Luke. How proud they had both been the day they'd signed the rental agreement! Regret burned in her heart. They'd taken immediate possession, but they had never managed to make their little house into a real home. Near tears, she pushed away from the table.

Luke grabbed her wrist, his thumb gently caressing the pulse point. "Let's go upstairs and make some better memories, Bonnie."

She shook her head. He didn't accept her denial. In one agile motion he stood and pulled her up with him. Taking her other wrist, he lifted her arms and locked them around his neck before enveloping her in his embrace. Her breathing was shallow as their bodies came together in a perfect fit.

Something old sparked something new, a fragile flame of restraint that heightened the anticipation. His mouth teased hers, sampling its sweetness without fully tasting of it. She parted her lips, inhaling his breath and feeling its warmth fill her senses. He fed his hunger with tender love bites, torturing her until she could take no more. Her breasts flattened against his hard chest as she pressed closer, demanding the satisfaction of his kiss.

"God!" he growled. "I want you so much, it hurts."

Wordlessly, Bonnie told Luke of her own consuming ache. She rose up on tiptoe and drew his head down. Her small show of aggression produced the results she desired.

Their mouths met and mated. His tongue sought her secrets, exploiting them with her consent. Her fingers weaved through his hair, its texture soft against her skin. Their deliciously heated exchange deepened into an act of love.

The kitchen clock cuckooed, its timing atrocious.

"The kids!" she remembered breathlessly.

"What?" he murmured into her mouth.

In a panic, she leaned away from his hard length and glanced toward the far wall. The mechanical bird squawked its last, then disappeared. If only she could disappear with it! "The kids—they're due back any minute."

"So?"

Bonnie broke free of his hold and fumbled to raise the camisole straps he'd deftly slipped off her shoulders. "What if they walked in on us?"

"We're not exactly strangers," he reminded her dryly.

Her guilty conscience provoked an angry tone. "We weren't setting a very sterling example for them, either."

"What happens between us is none of their damned business," he gritted. Frustration blazed unchecked in his eyes as he reached to embrace her again.

Bonnie dodged around the end of the table, eluding his arms. What a hypocrite she must seem—lecturing him yesterday about love versus lust, then melting in his arms today.

Tall, dark and clearly dissatisfied, Luke didn't appear readily inclined to forgive her lapse. Actually he looked rather ruthless, barring her access to the swinging doors to the dining room with his broad frame.

Just then, Dave's van wheezed into the drive alongside the house. Her legs went limp as wet noodles.

"This must be your lucky day, darlin'," Luke drawled. He stepped away from the swinging doors, allowing her safe passage from the kitchen. "I only hope you realize that you're getting off the hook a lot easier than you deserve."

Embarrassment stained her cheeks. Although she

didn't stand a chance of saving face, Bonnie squared her shoulders and started past him. As she reached out to push through the doors, Luke grabbed her arm and stopped her short.

"Next time," he warned, "I intend to see that you make good on your promises."

"Is that a threat?" she bristled.

"No." He released her. "That's a promise."

She blanched, knowing he meant business. Annoyed with both of them, she rushed out of the kitchen and ran upstairs.

It was an impossible situation, she mused while she showered. The two of them were like flint and stone—sparks flew everywhere when they came together. She took a jade-colored cotton jumpsuit out of her closet and zipped into it. How long before they created a fire that destroyed everyone around them, including Darlene and Dave?

"Next time." Bonnie repeated Luke's words as she tied an obi sash around her slender waist and brushed her hair into a golden silk cloud in front of the mirror.

There would be no next time. Drawing several deep breaths, Bonnie rehearsed the request she meant to make of Luke. He'd offered to return to Atlanta until Saturday, and she was going to take him up on it. What if he refused? Doubt pinched her features.

She studied her reflection soberly. It was speak now or hold her tongue and walk on eggs the rest of the week. She marched downstairs, her heart doing double-time.

Darlene had set the kitchen table and now stood staring out the window over the sink, watching Luke and Dave tending the grill on the brick patio.

"What's wrong?" Bonnie asked worriedly when her sister turned and exposed the tears streaming freely down her face.

"Nothing." Darlene smiled bashfully. "I was just thinking how happy mama and daddy would be to see the four of us together again, and . . ." She hiccuped and wiped her eyes with the back of her hand. "I'm sorry."

"Don't be silly." Bonnie's strength of purpose sputtered like a candle in the wind as she embraced her sister. "If it makes you feel better to cry, have at it."

Darlene buried her face in Bonnie's shoulder. "I was so afraid you wouldn't come home if you knew Luke would be here, too. But Dave insisted I tell you the truth and let you decide."

"Why, I wouldn't have missed your wedding for the world," Bonnie declared honestly. "You're all the family left to me."

When she raised her head, Darlene's eyes glowed with joy. "I'm so glad we could all be reunited like this."

"Me, too," Bonnie echoed faintly. Had she really said that?

Darlene hugged her fiercely, then let her go. "You'll just never know how much it means to Dave and me that you and Luke are spending this wonderful week with us."

Gritting her teeth, Bonnie managed the semblance of a smile.

"I'm going upstairs to take my bath," Darlene said, recovering her composure as she headed through the swinging doors. "Won't Dave be surprised when he sees me wearing your sundress?"

Alone in the kitchen, Bonnie removed the salad greens

from the refrigerator. She stood at the sink, stemming fresh spinach and slicing mushrooms. Though twilight tinted the world outside her window, she had no difficulty distinguishing Luke's masculine silhouette against the deep purple sky.

She couldn't ask him to leave; the kids would be crushed.

Luke swung an imaginary baseball bat with the grace of a natural athlete, and her heart soared with the rising moon. Why was it that the only man who stirred her was the same man who'd scarred her? He threw back his head, laughing at something she couldn't see, and her memory strayed to those innocent years when they'd shared every secret—whether silly or serious. She couldn't show him the door; she didn't want him to leave.

4

Dinner was simple yet superb. Luke had grilled their steaks to perfection, remembering without asking that Bonnie preferred hers medium rare. Crispy on the outside and butter-melting fluffy inside, his charcoaled potatoes were delicious. And everyone agreed that Bonnie's salad tasted as scrumptious as spring.

"I'm stuffed," Darlene groaned and pushed her plate away. "At the rate you two are feeding me, I'm going to outgrow my wedding dress before Saturday."

"Maybe it would help if you danced off a few of those extra calories," Dave suggested. "Why don't we all take a run out to the Hickory Tavern tonight?"

Bonnie's heart felt like it was shattering. The Hickory Tavern was the roadhouse where she had seen Luke with another woman before divorcing him. She studied her half-empty plate, acutely aware that Luke's eyes were on her.

"It sounds like fun, but I'm afraid I'll have to beg off," she declined, her voice stiffly polite. "You all go on without me, though. I've got plenty here to keep me occupied."

As if to prove she was far too busy for such frivolity, Bonnie stood and abruptly began clearing the table. Luke lit a cigarette and leaned back in his chair, its legs scraping the linoleum floor. His gaze never left her as she carried the dirty dishes to the sink.

"Oh, please, go with us," Darlene implored.

"We won't stay late," Dave promised.

Luke remained silent, as if he didn't care whether or not she went with them.

Bonnie shook her head vehemently while Dave and Darlene bombarded her with arguments, trying to convince her to change her mind. She'd never told anyone but her attorney and the judge why she had finally decided to divorce Luke. Relatives and friends had been left to draw their own conclusions, because she was too ashamed to admit that she wasn't woman enough to satisfy her man.

No. To return to the Hickory Tavern would be to revive her worst nightmare. The only difference was that this time she'd be walking in with her eyes wide open. Bonnie scrubbed the dishes with a vengeance, removing a bit more of their fading rose pattern in the process.

"What's the fun in dressing up if you can't go out and have fun with the people you love the most?" Darlene grumbled. The sundress she had borrowed was a bit loose in the bodice but fit her nicely otherwise. She adjusted the thin straps, then tossed her head. "Besides, Luke won't have anyone to dance with if you don't go."

Bonnie whirled away from the sink and met Luke's mildly amused expression. He knew *exactly* what she was thinking! Flicking soap bubbles off her fingertips, she shrugged indifferently. "Well, I've certainly never known him to lack for a partner."

His gaze narrowed noticeably, but he didn't utter a word in his own defense. Instead he stood, turned his back on the lot of them and strolled out of the kitchen.

How like him to leave her stuck with the explanations! Resentment bubbled through Bonnie's veins, but she bit her tongue. What purpose would it serve to air the reasons for her reluctance now?

"Tonight is probably our last chance to have some fun together before the wedding," Darlene said glumly. "Dave and I are leaving on our honeymoon right after the reception. And who knows for sure when you'll decide to come home again?"

Bonnie's resistance weakened. Darlene was becoming a regular pro at playing her heartstrings. "Give me fifteen minutes to change my clothes," she relented. "I'll go with you."

Darlene flashed a beguiling smile and tugged up the bodice of her dress. Dave hurried out of the kitchen to find Luke and inform him of the change in plans.

Upstairs, Bonnie studied the contents of her closet and wondered what to wear, then burst into peals of laughter. The Hickory Tavern hardly ranked as chic. In truth, it ~wed its questionable popularity to the fact that it was the only watering hole in town. She could probably wear a gunny sack and look perfectly at home!

The idea evoked another smile as she selected a plain blue halter top and a simple skirt that skimmed her knees. Without bothering to put on pantyhose, she slipped her feet into canvas espadrilles and applied a minimum of makeup. This was Darlene's night to shine, and she didn't intend to divert one beam of the spotlight to herself.

Ready with time to spare, Bonnie surveyed herself in the mirror. Too sexy, she criticized, peering over her shoulder at her bared back. Maybe she should swap the halter top for a blouse.

"Let's go!" Darlene rapped on the bedroom door just as she reached into her closet. "The guys are waiting in the van."

A honking horn confirmed the fact. With an impatient shrug at her own silliness, Bonnie hurried downstairs, halter top intact.

"You'll have to sit on the bed with Luke." Darlene waved her into the dark interior with an apologetic smile. "We took out the back seats in order to haul furniture."

Bonnie climbed in and groped her way toward the bed. Luke sat with his back against the rear door. His long, muscular legs were stretched across the narrow mattress while the shadows swathed his rugged features.

Perched on the edge of her makeshift seat, she was uncomfortably aware of his gaze trained on the bare skin she turned to him. As the van roared out of the driveway, she gripped the side-panel handle to maintain her balance. Neither of them spoke a word during the bumpy ride, which suited Bonnie just fine.

"Gosh, they're busy for a weeknight," Darlene said as Dave drove around the weathered gray building in search of a parking space. She turned and smiled brightly at Bonnie and Luke. "With so many people out howling tonight, you two are bound to run into some of your old friends."

The innocent remark stung Bonnie like a whiplash, and she inhaled sharply. *Old friends,* indeed! She caught her bottom lip between her teeth. Maybe she was blowing this all out of proportion, but the memory of Luke dancing with that redhead still pounded as violently as a jackhammer at her temples.

Luke slid forward on the mattress then, coming much too close for Bonnie's comfort. Unless she wanted to rub elbows and everything else with him, there was no place for her to go but up. She stood. At the same time the van swerved and she fell sideways, landing unceremoniously in Luke's lap.

"Drop-in company." He wrapped strong, welcoming arms around her slender waist. "I must say, it's my favorite kind."

"Save the sweet talk for your old friends." Her voice rasped with hurt despite her attempt to sound aloof.

"Were you jealous that night?" He tightened his embrace, as if trying to squeeze a confession from her.

"Of course not." She stubbornly refused to admit it aloud, even after all these years. "It was simply the last straw."

Luke frowned but his eyes were fathomless in the moonlight.

Bonnie turned her head, regretting the lie. How were they ever going to resolve their conflicts if she refused to discuss their marriage honestly? Why couldn't she just tell him the truth and be done with it? Angry with herself because she didn't know the answers to those difficult questions, she squirmed. "Let me go."

His hold slackened immediately. But as she started to rise, Dave slammed on the brakes. Luke grabbed her again and they tumbled backwards, Bonnie on top.

"Don't make any sudden moves with your left knee, or I'm ruined for life," he warned, his breath scorching her cheek.

Gingerly, Bonnie wiggled the leg he'd referred to and was mortified to discover it was snugly trapped between his lean thighs. They both groaned then, but for distinctly different reasons.

The front doors of the van opened and shut as Darlene and Dave made their exit.

"You dragged me down like this on purpose!" Bonnie accused.

"You used to enjoy this position."

"Damn you!" she gasped. "That was different."

"Delightfully so," Luke reminded her huskily.

Renewing her struggle, Bonnie tried wrenching free of his hold. Failing that, she glared down at him and repeated her earlier demand. "Let me go."

"Say *please*," Luke mocked, grinning wickedly as his hands roamed over her rib cage, setting her bare skin ablaze.

Sensations licked like fire through her veins when his thumbs brushed the sides of her breasts. She splayed her fingers across his powerful chest and whispered unsteadily, "Please."

Terminating their physical battle, he released her. Yet

she remained in place, a prisoner now of her own desires, every female inch of her keenly attuned to his hard, male shape. The embers of an age-old need flamed in her eyes.

Luke's gaze caught her fire and returned its golden radiance. He whispered her name, sending shivers down her spine. His hand caressed the nape of her neck before gently guiding her head lower. When their lips met, his tongue thrilled her mouth in a primitive rhythm of passion.

They rolled over, and Luke's hands slid down her body, taking their own sweet time while giving their own special pleasure. Bonnie raised her arms and wound them around his neck, holding him closer to her heart. His long fingers forged an erotic trail up her silky inner thigh toward the lacy, elastic leg of her—

Squealing tires and glaring headlights rudely invaded their privacy as a car pulled into the parking space beside the van. Luke lifted his head, muttering an oath under his breath. Beneath him, Bonnie stiffened as shame flooded through her with the force of a raging river. Whatever had possessed her to let things get so out-of-hand? Especially after this afternoon's fiasco in the kitchen!

They lay frozen on the lumpy mattress until slamming car doors and retreating footsteps echoed faintly in the night. As soon as she felt it was safe to do so, Bonnie scooted sideways and sat up.

Luke made no attempt to stop her; he simply propped himself up on one elbow and watched while she straightened her skirt and smoothed her hair with trembling hands.

"I'm sorry," she murmured when she'd collected the

tattered scraps of her self-control. Standing on shaky legs, she kept her head carefully averted. "That was a stupid stunt on my part. I swear it won't happen again."

"A lot of good that's going to do me now," he said harshly.

"I apologized and I meant it." Turning, she held out her hands, shakily beseeching his understanding. "If it's any consolation, I'm as frustrated as you are."

"Frustrated?" The tension that had seethed between them since yesterday erupted in his scornful remark. Luke's hand snaked out, encircling her wrist. "What a sophisticated vocabulary for a country girl."

"No, please, no," she begged as he pulled her toward the mattress, then dragged her down and onto her back.

"I warned you once today," he gritted. "Apparently my words fell on deaf ears."

"Wh-what are you doing?" she stammered when he straddled her waist with his knees and pinned her arms above her head.

"You showed me yours," he mocked, drawing one of her hands downward. "Now I'll show you mine."

"No!" Realizing his intention, she tried yanking her hand free of his iron grip. It was an exercise in futility, and she shut her eyes against his steely stare. "Stop it!"

Ignoring her order, he flattened her palm against him. "You don't frustrate me, Bonnie," he rasped. "You tear me up and turn me inside out."

Luke flung her hand away as if he couldn't bear her touch, then rolled off her writhing body. Ashamed of her own role in provoking the debasing incident, Bonnie lay with her eyes closed and listened while he slid the side-panel door open to leave the van.

She'd asked for it, pure and simple. He'd merely delivered. In a daze, she sat up and swung her legs over the side of the bed. They'd punished one another before with words and deeds, but never so brutally. *And never again,* she swore. Not if she could prevent it.

Rowdy laughter and loud music filtered across the graveled parking lot. The place was probably crawling with women who would love to finish what she'd started. Just imagining the scene that might greet her inside, she buried her face in her hands. Why, after all these years, did he still possess the power to hurt her?

Bonnie finally climbed out of the van, squared her shoulders and started walking toward the roadhouse. Although her back was ramrod stiff and her head high, she felt as vulnerable as a victim returning to the scene of the crime.

Big enough to oblige almost any urge, the Hickory Tavern was packed to the rafters. The plastic crack of a billiards break vied with the country and western music blasting from the corner jukebox. Dark, smoky and dank, the place was filled with men who had come to drink and chase women.

Bonnie paused in the doorway, unaware of the bold male glances and envious female glares appraising her. She scanned the blue-hazed barroom, seeking a familiar face. At this point, she thought grimly, even a recognizable rear view would do quite nicely.

"Hey, pretty lady, can I buy you a cool one?" A man dressed in his weeknight best pinned her against the door frame.

"Sorry, I'm with someone." She ducked under his

long arms, then sidestepped him. "Thank you, just the same."

His eyes inspected her thoroughly from head to toe, and she wondered whether he'd make trouble over her refusal. To his credit he bobbed his head and leaned casually against the door frame, ready to try his line on the next female arrival.

Bonnie stood on tiptoes and intensified her search. Even if Luke had decided to avoid her entirely for the rest of the evening, where had Darlene and Dave disappeared to? There was only one sure way to find out.

Plunging into the mob, she marveled at the number of people jammed into the tavern. She dodged a dangerous elbow and skirted a couple wrapped in a passionate embrace. Finally, after her eyes had adjusted to the dimness, she saw Darlene waving her over to a table near the dance floor.

"Wow!" Bonnie exclaimed as she took the chrome and vinyl chair beside her sister. "For a two-cent town, they sure turn out a dollar-bill crowd."

"It's because there's nowhere else to go around here." Darlene shrugged matter-of-factly. "Practically everybody living in Rebel's Ridge works in Atlanta." She took a chip from the basket on their table and dipped it into a bowl of fiery red sauce. "By the time people drive home and clean up, it's too late and too much trouble to backtrack forty miles for an evening's entertainment."

"Forgive me if I'm not impressed that this gin mill profits solely by convenience," Bonnie replied dryly. "Where's Dave?"

"Playing pool with one of the guys from work."

Darlene smiled indulgently and reached for another chip. "When I think he's lost enough money to last him awhile, I'll go collar him for a dance."

Bonnie glanced toward the far corner. Beneath a mushroom cloud of cigarette smoke, a dozen men huddled around the pool table. Judging from the ribald remarks and raucous laughter, Dave was holding his own. She looked away. If Luke had been there, he would have stood head and shoulders above the rest.

A curvaceous waitress wearing skintight jeans and a T-shirt stopped at the table. Darlene ordered a beer. Although she normally drank wine spritzers, Bonnie requested the same.

The rockabilly music rendered ordinary conversation impossible, and Darlene seemed perfectly content to sit and sip. Bonnie surveyed the dance floor where several couples moved in time to the music, and where she half-expected to spot Luke with another woman in tow.

He wasn't there, and her heart plummeted. Maybe he'd come in the front door and latched onto a willing one-night fling, then ducked out the back door with her. Perhaps . . . her imagination ran rampant, yet she kept her features pleasantly composed.

What right did she have to be jealous? Thanks to their divorce, Luke was free to indulge himself in any fashion he pleased. If he wanted to ring the chimes of every southern belle he met, he was certainly entitled. *She* didn't care.

Yes, she did. Damn the quibbling, she cared. But she'd been running scared for so many years, she didn't know how to stop. Not even for Luke. A haunting ballad on the jukebox echoed her desolation as she sipped her beer, feigning indifference. She'd never felt more alone in her life.

"As I live and breathe, it's Bonnie!"

Bonnie glanced up into twinkling blue eyes that she instantly recognized, then stood.

"Sueanne!" She embraced her oldest and dearest friend, whom she hadn't seen in seven years. "I tried to return your call today, but I didn't get an answer."

Sueanne, who was obviously pregnant, patted her abdomen and grinned. "It takes me twelve rings to get from our backyard to the telephone these days."

"I hung up after ten," Bonnie admitted. She looked down and laughed. "What's a mother-to-be doing in *this* disreputable place?"

"It beats sitting home watching reruns on the tube."

"And where's Tom?" Bonnie glanced around for her friend's husband. "I'd love to see him while I'm home."

"He's in the parking lot showing our new pickup truck to Luke," the other woman answered.

Bonnie winced and gave herself a swift mental kick for automatically having misjudged the reason for his absence.

Sueanne smiled wryly. "Honestly, Tom is worse than a little boy—he couldn't stand to have his toy sit unnoticed in the driveway all night."

"Why don't you join the hen party?" Bonnie invited, turning her attention back to her friend. She squeezed Sueanne's shoulders affectionately. "How are you?"

"As comfortable as possible, considering it's twins."

"Twins!" Bonnie laughed uncertainly. "Dare I offer my congratulations?"

"In duplicate." Sueanne smiled serenely, her eyes

radiating a contentment that Bonnie envied to the core of her soul. "I grumble some, but I wouldn't trade places with anyone I know."

"Sit in my chair, Sueanne," Darlene insisted. She grabbed another chip, then pushed away from the table. "I'm going to put a headlock on Dave and drag him onto the dance floor before I founder myself on junk food." She stood, pulled up the bodice of Bonnie's sundress and turned in the direction of the pool table. "Besides, I'm sure you two have a lot of catching up to do after all these years."

Sueanne lowered herself cautiously into the vacated chair, sighing when she was comfortably situated. "I always resemble a beached whale beginning about my seventh month."

"Nonsense," Bonnie refuted in a wistful tone. "You look terrific." The pain of her own long-ago loss wrenched her heart, yet she felt a vicarious joy in her friend's obvious sense of well-being. "How many will this make?"

"Four. Our oldest starts preschool this fall, and the youngest has been toddling since Christmas." She winced and pressed a hand to her swollen side. "Judging from their prenatal activities, these two will be born wearing track shoes."

When the waitress stopped again, Bonnie shook her head, refusing a second beer, and Sueanne ordered a glass of water with a twist of lime. Mercifully, someone lowered the volume on the jukebox and the women were able to talk quietly.

"Life as a northerner sounds hectic," Sueanne remarked. "It must make Rebel's Ridge seem awfully dull."

"Not really." The words were out before Bonnie realized it. She shrugged. "I've met lots of famous people through my catering service, which is fun if their egos aren't overinflated. And while New York presents incomparable cultural opportunities, the quality of life here is much better—at least in my opinion."

"Give me a for instance," Sueanne prompted.

"Okay. There's no feeling of space in New York—no breathing room, so to speak. I have to live in the city because of my business. And when I look out my windows, instead of trees or fields of clover all I see is other buildings." Bonnie wrinkled her nose. "In a lot of corny ways, I suppose I'm still a country girl at heart."

"There's nothing wrong with that." Sueanne smiled expectantly. "Are you seeing anyone special?"

"I date." Bonnie didn't expand on her answer. If she admitted that no other man she'd met could hold a candle to Luke, she'd sound like the original lovesick fool. She changed the subject before Sueanne could pursue it. "How's Tom?"

"Now that he's adjusted to the idea he'll be supporting enough people to start his own basketball team, he's fine." Her expression pensive, Sueanne tucked an auburn strand of hair behind her ear. "He works for Luke."

"So I've heard." Bonnie waved to Darlene, who'd succeeded in luring Dave away from the pool table and onto the dance floor.

An awkward silence punctuated their conversation. In years past, Bonnie would have poured out her heart to Sueanne. But Sueanne's marriage to one of Luke's employees effectively precluded such a personal discussion. It wouldn't be fair to impose on her friend's loyalties. If push came to shove, it was only natural that she'd consider her family's welfare first.

"Luke is a good man." Sueanne's uncanny intuition proved sharper than ever. She leaned forward as far as her protruding abdomen would permit. "And I'm not saying that just because he's Tom's boss, either."

"I know." Bonnie sighed distractedly. "This would all be so much easier if he'd only had the decency to grow fat and bald while I was gone."

"Now who's spouting nonsense?" Sueanne chided softly. "I'll agree Luke is a handsome devil—virtually a walking magnet where women are concerned. But that's not the reason you fell head-over-heels for him, and I seriously doubt that's why you're in such a quandary now."

"I *am* confused," Bonnie said. "But as desperately as I might need a sounding board, I wouldn't dream of jeopardizing Tom's job or throwing a monkey wrench into your marriage."

"Poppycock." Sueanne reached over and grasped Bonnie's hands between her own. "Remember, we graduated from double-Dutch ice cream into double-A bras together. And in spite of the fact we've lost contact the past seven years, I still think of you as my best friend. If you need it, my ear is yours for the bending."

"Thanks, Sueanne." Bonnie glanced around and grinned. "This is hardly the time or place for true confessions. But if things get any more tangled than they already are, you may well find me bawling like a baby on your doorstep."

"Anytime." Sueanne released her hands and reached for her water glass.

"Say, don't I know you?" An obviously intoxicated stranger leaned over the table and stared intently at Bonnie.

"I don't think so." She averted her face from the sour-mash odor of his breath. "Maybe you've confused me with someone else."

"No." The brash intruder flattened his palms on the tabletop, struggling to stay upright. "I've seen you before —I'm sure of it. What's your name?"

She shook her head, refusing to oblige him. From the corner of her eye, she saw Sueanne's shoulders shaking with laughter.

"Tell me your name." Weaving precariously, he bent closer.

Bonnie slid her chair sideways until she ran into the iron railing that separated the bar area from the dance floor. Gritting her teeth, she muttered a vehement "Damn!"

"Pam?" He drew back a bit, clearly baffled. "Pam," he repeated. "Funny, it doesn't ring a bell."

Men! she fumed. First, Luke had left her in suspense by pulling a vanishing act that Houdini would have envied. Now this . . .

"C'mon, Pam." He grabbed her hand. "Let's dance."

Bonnie yanked free, accidentally throwing him off-balance. Horrified, she watched as he toppled to the floor and dragged an unoccupied chair from the neighboring table over on top of him. Someone unplugged the jukebox, and the roadhouse fell curiously and ominously silent.

"What the hell—" Luke shouldered his way through the people.

Hot on his heels, Tom rushed to where Sueanne sat laughing uncontrollably, tears streaming down her face.

Luke glanced at Bonnie. Then, apparently satisfied that she was unharmed, he clenched his fists and glared toward the floor.

Once, twice, the man blinked his bloodshot eyes. Floundering like a fish out of water, he grappled impotently with the heavy metal chair. When Bonnie reached out to help, he cringed.

A crowd gathered, thirsting for a brawl to chase their beers.

"Teach him a lesson, Luke," someone goaded.

"Knock him into the next county," another suggested.

Bonnie froze, a wave of pity washing through her for the cowering figure on the floor. *Enough!* she wanted to scream. Yet she waited with everyone else, fear churning inside her.

Luke looked at her, his expression an unreadable meld of emotions. He tossed the chair aside, and her heart stopped beating. When he offered the fallen man a hand up, she almost wept with relief.

The rather belligerent crowd dispersed reluctantly. Bonnie wanted to slap some common sense into each and every one of them. Instead she said good-bye to Sueanne and reassured her anxious sister while Luke arranged a ride home for the unfortunate victim of her brush-off.

"Come on, Calamity Jane." Luke took her hand in his. "They're playing our song."

"I don't hear any music." But she stood and followed him.

"You will." He smiled mysteriously.

"Oh?" she challenged.

"I gave Darlene a handful of change and told her to punch a certain slow number." His dark gaze drifted downward. "Something to soothe her sister's savage breast."

Her breath caught in her throat when he focused on the front of her halter top. True to Luke's prediction, *their* old song flowed softly from the jukebox. He slipped his arms around her slim waist; she raised her hands to his broad shoulders. Their bodies merged, and she felt the strong drum of his heartbeat against hers as they swayed in smooth, sensuous harmony.

"Luke," she whispered hesitantly, "I *was* jealous that night—insanely so." Bonnie tipped her head back. Expecting to see triumph in his eyes, she marveled at finding something like pain clouding their depths.

"If it makes you feel any better, I got dead drunk after you threw your ring in my face. I passed out on her sofa before anything happened, and she took her scissors to my clothes." He grimaced comically. "I woke up the next morning sicker than sin and had to drive home in my birthday suit."

She looked at him, her lips softly parted, and smiled. "You deserved it."

"I did," he agreed softly, nuzzling her ear.

Their steps grew smaller as they drew closer. Bonnie wrapped her arms tightly around his neck while Luke's hands caressed her bare back, spreading a slow, honeyed heat. She whispered his name when his mouth brushed her temple, and they sealed their exquisite awareness of each other with a kiss that didn't end with the music.

The sound of shuffling feet and a mild cough broke

them apart. Dave's embarrassment shone bright as a beacon on his freckled face, despite the dim lighting. "I hate to interrupt your, ah, discussion, but Darlene and I are going to a party."

Luke traced the angle of Bonnie's cheek with his forefinger. "Sounds like fun."

Dave reached into his jeans pocket, fished out the keys to his van and handed them over. "You can take my wheels whenever you're ready to leave here. We've already got a ride to and from the party."

"Fine." Luke waited until Dave was gone, then dangled the keys in her face. "It's your decision, babe. Do we hit the road or do we dance till dawn?"

Bonnie's heart made up her mind. If it was wrong to need him, she didn't want to be right. Not tonight. She leaned against his chest, almost purring with anticipation. "Frankly, my feet are killing me."

5

Their haste to leave the Hickory Tavern bordered on the indecent. While Bonnie grabbed her purse off the table, Luke shoved a twenty-dollar bill at the waitress and told her to keep the change. Before the happily surprised woman finished sputtering her thanks, they were halfway to the door.

They rode home wrapped in a silken web of silence. A white chocolate moon chased them every mile along the rural backroad.

Curled up in the captain's seat on the passenger side, Bonnie captured Luke's bold male profile on her heart's canvas. She memorized each detail—the sexy slant of his deep-set eyes, the sharply sculptured nose and full mouth.

He swung the van into the driveway and parked beside

a lush bank of lilacs. A fragile urgency quickened their steps as they walked hand-in-hand toward the wide-planked porch. He opened the front door, then slowed the tempo when he turned and took her in his warm embrace.

"Welcome home," he murmured.

"I've missed you," she admitted.

Luke tipped her chin and traced the outline of her lips with his thumb. "Show me. Show me what we have together."

It was more than an invitation of the flesh. It was a beautiful lie that bound them again, but only for a little while.

Bonnie raised her hand and touched his mouth, relearning its texture. A soft cry escaped her when his tongue touched the sensitive pads of her fingertips.

"God, you feel good." He crushed her to him, molding her legs, her hips, her breasts to the burning length of his body.

A terrible ache filled her heart. This week was all they had before they went their separate ways. Bonnie closed her eyes to the future, blotting out everything but the present.

"Let's go inside." Luke scooped her into his arms and carried her over the threshold, toward the stairway. "Otherwise, the neighbors across the road will have one hell of a tale to tell tomorrow."

"Modesty certainly becomes you," she teased, wrapping her arms around his neck while he lithely climbed the stairs. "I can remember when you were so anxious to have me, you didn't care who might know."

"You weren't exactly averse to taking chances, either,"

he challenged. "I'll never forget that Saturday afternoon you dragged me out to the circle—"

"*Dragged* you?" She feigned an insulted tone. "I thought I was going to have a heart attack running to keep up with you."

"All right," he conceded, pausing in mid-stride to open the bedroom door. "You *suggested* we take a walk." His laughter rumbled deeply. What a beautiful sound! "About ten minutes after we got there, your dad started mowing the meadow with that damned tractor—"

"You jumped back into your jeans so fast, I figured you were snake-bit," Bonnie recalled with a smile. "There I was, naked as a newborn, my father roaring up the hill on his riding mower—"

"Talk about a narrow escape," Luke reminisced wryly. "If he'd caught us, he'd have made bone meal out of me in no time flat."

They laughed together, and Bonnie felt a soaring sense of freedom in their total accord. She'd never belonged to any man but Luke; she never would.

"I don't think we ever fooled my folks or your mother for a minute, though." She rumpled his thick hair and thrilled to his flexing muscles as he let her feet slide slowly to the floor. "None of them acted the least bit surprised when we told them we'd eloped."

Unbidden tears stung her eyes then, and she lowered her lashes. Despite the circumstances prompting the marriage, her parents had readily, proudly accepted Luke as their son-in-law. Bonnie's stomach fluttered and her fingers fumbled clumsily as she tried to unfasten the front button at the waistband of her skirt.

"Don't rush it, darling." Luke laid a steadying hand

over hers, as if he sensed the reason for her sudden show of sadness. "I miss all of them, too. Your folks always treated me like one of their own, even after I gave them good cause not to."

He drew her into his arms and hugged her fiercely, shutting out the pain that threatened to intrude on their privacy. The smell of Cape jasmine spiced the breeze wafting through the window screen, and a cricket chirped for its mate in the night. Bonnie rested her tear-stained cheek against his solid chest, absorbing his strength and treasuring the fact that he was temporarily hers.

"I wanted to kill that creep tonight." A violent note edged his voice, but she wasn't afraid. He cupped her face between his callused palms, holding her in a gentle grip. "But when you looked at me, something told me that if I so much as mussed a hair on his sweaty head, I'd wind up the loser."

"Welcome to my corner, champ," she whispered.

"I never left your corner, Bonnie," he stated simply.

She hushed him with a kiss. Talk like that only led to tears. "I'm going to take a bath," she announced.

"Can I wash your back?" His hands made mesmerizing circles along her spine.

Bonnie nodded, hypnotized by his touch.

Luke grinned wickedly. "Can I wash your front?"

"Only if I can wash yours," she answered coyly.

"Lady, you just struck a deal," he declared.

Arm-in-arm, they walked into the connecting bathroom. She turned the faucets on full and poured a heaping capful of scented crystals into the warm, rushing water.

Shyly, as if it were the first time, Bonnie undressed for him. Dropping her clothes where she stood, she was keenly aware of Luke's velvety gaze on the skin she bared. Her pulse raced wildly; it mattered so much that she please him. She held her breath and raised her head. The volcanic passion in his eyes dissolved her doubts.

"My memory didn't serve me well enough," he observed huskily. Luke had stripped to the waist, then stopped to watch her disrobe. "If you don't get into that tub, pronto, you aren't going to get a bath until sometime tomorrow."

She stepped over the porcelain edge, turned off the tap and sank down into the bubbly water. "Last one in has to mop up later."

Luke lost, but both of them were winners. He shed his clothes, then climbed in and sat facing her. She knelt between his legs, allowing him any liberty he enjoyed.

With unhurried hands he lathered her breasts, his circular motion creating an exquisite friction that left her tingling from scalp to toes. Then he reached beneath the bubbles and scooped up clear water to rinse away the soap. When he leaned forward and sipped from the streams he'd made on her skin, she arched reflexively against him. "You taste so good," he murmured. "You always tasted good—all over."

His mouth savored each curve, each swell while he bathed her body with love. Suddenly, Luke lifted her higher as his hands moved lower, touching her tenderly. Bonnie splayed her fingers across his shoulders, seeking support. Caught up in a current she couldn't fight, she drifted with the wet and wonderful sensations rippling through her. He held her tight until her storm was spent, then helped her glide down into the water.

"My turn," he rasped.

"My pleasure."

Bonnie soaped him slowly, starting with his wide shoulders. She massaged his muscular, hair-matted chest and stroked the sensitive area under his arms before her hands slipped below the waterline.

His pure animal groan increased both her boldness and the amount of pressure she applied. She wanted him to scale the same dizzying heights where she'd soared earlier, but he would only let her take him half the way.

"I won't go without you," he decreed hoarsely.

"I'm ready whenever you are," she whispered.

In better control than his ragged breathing implied, Luke grasped her wrists and wrapped her arms around his neck. Raising himself up on his knees, he brought her into full contact with his upper torso before he stood and lifted her out of the tub. They toweled each other dry, pausing occasionally for soft kisses or arousing nibbles that left new beads of moisture.

Luke carried her into the bedroom and laid her gently on the feather mattress. Then, silently as a dream, he came to bed.

"The light . . ." Bonnie pointed to the lamp on the dresser.

"Leave it on," he urged. "I want to see if you remember me."

She did. Her body anticipated his every intimate request and answered with one of its own. His breath spilled warm as wine on her satiny skin as his kisses rained along her delicate collarbone, over the luscious swell of her rib cage, then to lower pulse points sheltered in secret silken places.

When she cried his name, Luke shifted his weight and moved up, sliding his muscled legs between her thighs. Bonnie felt his heart beating beneath her hands, and every vestige of mistrust melted in the consuming heat of her need. She arched her hips to meet the thrust of his, then bit back a cry of mingled pleasure and pain. He was instantly aware of why she tensed and ecstatic disbelief flared in his lazy-lidded eyes.

"Bonnie." He stopped, searching her flushed face.

"Love me, Luke," she pleaded softly.

"I do," he vowed, "more than I can tell you."

"Show me," she whispered.

He did. Luke pillowed her head in the hollow of his shoulder, and Bonnie pressed her lips to that rippling ridge of muscle. Cradling her in the most intimate embrace, he rocked her with the force of his love. Together again, they satisfied a sterling promise untarnished by time.

Much later, they lay entwined while the night-perfumed air fanned their bodies. They slept spoon-fashion, tucked in a tight curl, and she knew she was truly home. But only for a little while.

A splintering crash, followed in short order by a good-natured curse and rowdy laughter, woke her.

Stretching luxuriously, she basked in a morning-after glow so rosy, it shamed the sunshine streaming through the window. She shouldn't feel this good, this complete, this alive. But she did.

That Luke's side of the bed was empty didn't worry

her a whit. He'd be back. A knowing smile toyed at her lips when Bonnie rolled over and hugged his pillow, inhaling the male scent lingering in the soft, cotton case.

In the bright light of day she didn't regret what had happened. Lying here, waiting for Luke to return, felt more natural than anything she'd done in years. A frown turned her smile upside down. She shouldn't think along those lines, knowing their time together was so short.

The bedroom door creaked as Luke shouldered it open. His hands were full, a mug of steaming coffee gripped in each one. The sight of him, clad only in faded jeans, the shadow of a night's growth evident on his lean cheeks, tugged at her heart.

His image blurred before her eyes. After last night, she didn't want to leave him. But she would. And for his sake as well as hers, it was probably best that she never return.

"Sorry if the noise woke you." Luke kicked the door closed behind him.

Blinking back the tears, Bonnie propped herself up on one elbow. "What *was* that awful crash, anyway?"

"Dave is helping Darlene clean out the buffet so they can move it into Atlanta today." Luke paused and smiled. "It's quite a show down there, literally like watching a bull turned loose in a china shop."

She laughed and watched him approach the bed.

"Hey, I like what you're wearing." He towered over her, his dark gaze provocatively skimming her curves, which were covered only by the sheet.

"I selected it with you in mind." Bonnie shifted positions and let the sheet fall away, providing him with an unrestricted view of her nude figure.

"If you ever decide to try for the 'best undressed' list,

you've got my vote." Luke placed the cups on the nightstand, then the mattress sagged as he lowered himself beside her. "What do you want for breakfast?"

"I'll give you three guesses." Her hands slowly traced the pattern of hair on his muscular chest, down to his flat stomach. "And the first two don't count."

"Sunnyside up?" he asked huskily.

"Hard-boiled," she whispered.

Bonnie's eyes revealed the same warmth that was smoldering in his. Luke's mouth hovered a fraction of an inch away from her parted lips and, for a precious instant, nothing else existed for her but him. It had always been this way between them; it always would. Seven years times seven couldn't alter the heat of their passion.

He stood and stripped off his jeans before joining her in bed. Her fingers feathered softly across his virile features, weaved a wanton love dance through his thick hair and curved possessively around his corded neck.

Luke let her set the pace and seemed to understand what she said with her silence. Bonnie drew him down and took him into her, needing this next new memory more desperately than the ones they'd made last night.

She held him captive until he freed her. Their mouths fused and their fingers laced as they found release where they'd left it, with each other.

Later, they sipped cool coffee and snuggled beneath the sheets. And they talked, revealing bits and pieces of their separate professional lives while studiously avoiding any personal issues that might spark an argument.

Because Luke seemed genuinely interested, Bonnie told him how she'd come to launch her catering service in a rented Manhattan storefront. She'd risked her entire savings account on her culinary talent after resigning from an assistant chef's position at the elegant restaurant where she had worked while attending night school. Making light of the trials, she focused instead on the small triumphs and modest achievements in her transition from country girl to successful entrepreneur.

In turn, Luke recounted his own transformation from toolbox laborer to general contractor to president of a construction company with over one hundred million dollars' worth of work in progress in Atlanta alone.

"Do you realize how many parallels there are in our stories?" Bonnie pressed her lips to the tanned column of his throat and felt his fingers threading through her tawny hair. "Both of us started with nothing, so to speak—"

"Nothing but pride for a slave driver," Luke interrupted bitterly. There was a closed look about him when she raised her head to see his face. "We had made a mess of our marriage. I think we both unconsciously decided we couldn't afford two failures in a row."

"Maybe you're right," she agreed sadly, resting her head on his chest. His theory made perfect sense, but it also destroyed the intimate mood they'd managed to maintain following their lovemaking.

"Of course I'm right." Luke lifted her chin, forcing her to meet his disturbingly dark gaze. "There are two kinds of people in this world, Bonnie—those who cave in when they founder, and those who use their failure in one area as a tool to carve out success in another."

"Naturally, we fall into the second category," she murmured, wounded by his implication that if they'd stayed married, they would have remained impoverished.

"You and I are a lot alike." Luke's pragmatic tone wreaked havoc with her heart. "When the going got rough, we were tough enough to make hard decisions and difficult choices. We both faced up to no-win situations and won anyway."

"We ought to wear our blue ribbons to bed." Bonnie's voice quivered with hurt. She sat up with extreme care and moved away from Luke. "God knows, neither of us wants to make the mistake of sleeping with a loser."

He grabbed her wrist as she slid toward the edge of the mattress, trapping her before she escaped. "Look at me," he ordered. When she did, he regarded her with a probing gaze. "You haven't had sex since our divorce."

She knew her flush was all the confirmation he required.

"Why?" he demanded.

Bonnie closed her eyes and sighed. For reasons she didn't completely understand, she had hoped to avoid discussing this. Somehow, though, she'd lost control of the situation—a pattern with her where Luke was concerned. "It wasn't for lack of opportunity," she asserted. "I've refused my share of invitations."

"What stopped you? You always enjoyed making love."

"At first I was scared," she admitted, "so saying no just became second nature to me." She smiled ruefully. "About the time I got brave enough to consider taking the big plunge, my catering service was booked solid. Something had to give—in this instance, my social life."

"Damn!" Luke's oath was rife with self-disgust. "I must have done a real hatchet job on your ego for you to deny yourself a normal love life for seven years."

Bonnie flashed him a proud look. "If the fact that I haven't won a gold medal in the sexual olympics makes me abnormal, then so be it."

Fine threads of tension entangled her nerves. Would her ex-husband, a contemporary man, ridicule her old-fashioned code of morality? She remembered Darlene mentioning not too long ago that he was dating a woman named Chris Miller, someone from his circle of professional acquaintances. Bonnie hadn't pressed for details, and her one personal wish for the week was that she wouldn't have to meet his latest flame.

It suddenly seemed urgent that Luke hear the whole truth, although she hesitated to delve too deeply into her own heart for the cause of her concern. Leaning across the bed, she stroked the carved angle of his jawline. "I've met a lot of nice men since I left here. I've just never met another man I wanted to sleep with."

His broad chest heaved with a deep breath. "Bonnie—"

Crash! The horrible noise reverberated like a cannon shot from downstairs, shattering their privacy.

"What the—" Luke leaped out of bed and made a mad dash toward the bedroom door.

"Aren't you forgetting something?" she called after him, her eyes shining with amusement.

Luke stopped short of yanking the door open, glanced down at himself, then smiled sheepishly. Delighted laughter burst from Bonnie as he did an abrupt about-face and hurried back to retrieve his jeans.

"I hope Dave has more finesse as a bridegroom than he's shown as a moving man," Luke grumbled as he dressed. "I can just picture him dropping poor Darlene when he carries her across the threshold."

"Maybe his big brother ought to have a talk with him," Bonnie suggested in a teasing voice. She rose from the bed and walked to the closet, where she selected a striped halter dress. "Or, if worse comes to worst, you can rent a wheelbarrow and spare Darlene the danger of being bounced into the bridal suite."

"Hey, there's no need for you to get dressed, too," Luke protested when he noticed what she was doing. "I'll just run down and help them load the buffet into Dave's van, then come right back up here."

"We're going grocery shopping today," she said, dangling lacy bikini panties and a half-slip from her index finger. "Remember?"

"Suit yourself," he conceded as he opened the door. "But what I had in mind is a hell of a lot more fun than snapping beans and squeezing tomatoes."

Bonnie started toward the bathroom, then paused in the doorway, suddenly self-conscious about the fact that Darlene and Dave would know she and Luke had spent last night and the better part of this morning in bed together. "Do you suppose there's any chance the kids would believe it if we told them I overslept?"

"Nope," he mocked dryly.

Vividly aware of her nudity and the almost physical touch of his midnight gaze on her skin, she felt totally vulnerable.

His measuring look increased her agitation. "Why do you keep referring to Darlene and Dave as kids when they're actually adults?"

"Habit, I suppose." She shrugged, disconcerted.

"Well, as adults who are about to be married," he continued levelly, "I'm sure they're both educated about the facts of life."

Bonnie's expression betrayed her. Until this moment, it hadn't occurred to her that Darlene and Dave might be . . . "Are you suggesting—"

"I don't know, and I haven't asked because I respect their privacy." He nailed her in place with a hard stare. "You seem to forget that they're older and considerably more settled than we were when we eloped."

Inwardly she reeled, as if he'd hit her with a brickbat. Her nerves, already strained, were at the breaking point. "You failed to mention their other advantage—they're marrying because they *want* to, not because they *have* to."

"I told you the other night that I'm through tormenting myself over our mistakes." Anger darkened his eyes. "If you choose to remain a prisoner of the past, that's certainly your privilege. But I granted myself a pardon the day you cashed my check and climbed on that northbound bus."

"How fortunate that you were able to write me off so easily." An intense pain twisted cruelly inside her as she mustered what little dignity he'd left her. "For a little while, I'd forgotten why I divorced you. Thanks for reminding me of what a heartless bastard you really are."

The cold glitter in his eyes chilled her to the bone. "Did you ever stop to think that might be a two-way street?"

She hadn't, of course. Bonnie froze, trying to get a grip on her emotions. "Too bad we missed the detour signs," she whispered tautly, "it would have saved us another head-on collision."

Choking back a sob, she stepped into the bathroom and slammed the door behind her. She'd already surrendered her body and soul. Damned if she'd give him the satisfaction of seeing her cry!

6

~∞∞∞∞∞∞∞∞~

Bonnie didn't cry. Tears wouldn't solve her problems or gain her a moment's peace of mind. Besides, one more weeping fit and she would be a prime candidate for salt tablets.

She showered, shaved her legs to a smooth sheen, and shampooed her hair to a squeaky-clean shine. And she applied makeup—lots of it. After all, she'd paid a fortune for these little bottles of perfumed confidence. Why not use them to her best advantage?

Bonnie studied her reflection in the mirror and saw living proof that there was no future in conducting inquests over past mistakes. Luke was right. She had to forgive herself.

She tied up the straps of her halter dress, slipped on a pair of smart leather flats, spritzed a cloud of her favorite fragrance into the air and walked through it when she left the bedroom. Knowing that her destination was finally the right one, she moved with new purpose.

Yesterday was gone and tomorrow might never come. Today, she was going to stop looking back with regret and start looking ahead with hope.

Luke stood on the front porch bidding farewell to Darlene, Dave and the dining room buffet. Bonnie waited inside, watching him through the bay window. Showered and clean-shaven, he wore a blue cotton sailing shirt, neatly pressed jeans and moccasin-style loafers.

He laughed at something Dave said, and the booming joy of it echoed like a bass drum in her ears. He shrugged those broad shoulders, and her stomach contracted at his unconscious show of strength. When he turned to enter the house, she nearly bolted; she was so edgy. Why hadn't she just shinnied down the tree outside her bedroom window this morning and stowed away in the silverware drawer?

Bonnie's pulse skittered frantically when the screen door slammed shut behind him. Luke stopped abruptly in the entryway as soon as he spotted her frozen in place beside the front window. Their gazes met, and the silence was filled with electric tension.

"I'm sorry—" he began.

"I'm sorry—" she said.

They both broke off as they spoke. He grinned. She smiled. It eased her tension considerably.

"Go ahead," he insisted.

"You first," she urged.

Luke chuckled. "At least we're on the same wavelength." He waited quietly, patiently, as if he realized that she was engaged in a very personal and important struggle.

She stared down at the threadbare moss-green carpet without actually seeing it. How could she best convince him that she was breaking the mold of self-blame and freeing herself, finally, of the pain? Now that she needed them, where were all those magical words that she'd thought of while still upstairs?

She looked up and licked her lips, which had gone dry despite the generous coat of gloss that she'd applied. He tipped his head slightly, and the morning sun lit the virile contours of his face. Bonnie braved another smile. Luke returned it.

Suddenly a marvelous wave of relief crested inside her. In some ways, this man knew her better than she knew herself. Even if her declaration of emotional independence was phrased in less than eloquent terms, he would understand exactly what she meant.

"Have you noticed yet?" Arms outstretched, she twirled around twice. "I'm not wearing my hair shirt anymore."

He eliminated the distance between them in a few limber strides and caught her in a loving embrace. Holding her fiercely, as if afraid she might escape, he captured her mouth with his and celebrated the moment with a tenderness that left her trembling.

They drew slightly apart but kept their arms tightly locked around one another. For now, this was enough.

"Listen—" he began.

"I'm all ears," she teased.

"Oh, yeah?" Shrewdly shifting his gaze, Luke peered down the V-neck of her halter dress.

"None of that," Bonnie whispered.

Luke's expression grew serious then. "I never dreamed, what with your being gone so long—" He reached out and smoothed her hair away from her face, his dark brows furrowing together. "It never occurred to me last night or this morning either, although it should have . . ." He shrugged, clearly irritated with himself and asked her point-blank, "What if you're pregnant again?"

"I'm not," she answered honestly.

His nostrils flared. "But—"

She pressed her fingertips to his mouth. "We should have discussed this sooner. The last time we threw caution to the wind, it blew trouble in our faces."

He nodded, his gaze narrowing slightly.

"Remember what I told you this morning about finally being ready to take the big plunge?" she prompted.

He nodded again, studying her steadily.

She lowered her hand and smiled reassuringly. "Well, you'll be pleased to hear that my preparations included a visit to my friendly neighborhood physician."

Luke gaped at her for a full second, then spun and struck a brisk pace toward the door. Bonnie stood stupidly, wondering if she'd only imagined that suspicious look in his eyes. Was he upset because she was protected, for heaven's sake? Surely he hadn't expected her to take a *second* risk?

Determined to clear the air, she started after him. When he stopped and turned, she slammed into his hard chest. He gripped her upper arms, half-steadying, half-shaking her.

"All right, I admit it!" Raw emotion choked his voice. "For one ridiculous instant, I wished I'd made you pregnant."

It was Bonnie's turn to gape.

Luke heaved a sigh and let her go. "If you're willing to accept a plea of temporary insanity on my part and forget I said that, I'll run you into Atlanta."

Stunned, she watched him walk away. Her jaw felt like it had suddenly come unhinged. He held the screen door open for her. She grabbed her purse off the small vestibule chest and rushed past him.

"Your lipstick is smeared," he muttered fondly.

She glanced up and couldn't help but smile. "So is yours."

The door banged shut as he wiped the glossy evidence of their kiss off his mouth with the back of his hand. Her steps slowed as she crossed the porch and recognized the truck parked in the driveway.

"The Miser's Dream!" she whooped in delight, then ran down the steps toward the gleaming black pickup that he'd purchased at an auction the summer he'd turned sixteen. "Where have you been keeping it?"

"I loaned it to Sueanne and Tom while they were waiting for delivery of their new truck," he explained, joining her in the driveway. "Tom promised last night that he'd drop it by this morning on his way to work."

Luke's pickup had been the bargain of the century—a twenty-five-dollar steal! Bonnie rubbed her hand along the hood, remembering well what a rusty, seat-sprung heap it had been before he'd restored it. All that summer, she and every other kid in town had watched him sand it by hand and clean it inside and out. He had spraypainted it—twenty cans' worth, if she recalled correctly—then had the final coat applied professionally, paying for it with money he had earned sacking groceries at the general store.

Mischief twinkled in his eyes. "Do you realize this old buggy will qualify for antique license plates before too long?"

She grimaced. "Don't tell me that! It makes me feel like I should run right out and stock up on support hose and hairnets."

Luke laughed boisterously as he opened the passenger door. When she climbed into the spanking-clean cab, he closed the door and braced his chin on the partially lowered window. He regarded her intently as the teasing light faded from his eyes. "Do you remember when keeping the gas tank filled was the second most important thing to us?"

How could she forget? Lord, she'd carried those memories like scars! Bonnie sat primly, hands folded in her lap, while a scalding blush betrayed her outward composure.

Just how many rainy nights had they parked in the willow stand near Tucker's Creek, proving their love in awkward positions which had left stick-shift shaped bruises on very private parts? A poignant smile curved her lips as she ran a hand over the durable herringbone upholstery. To this day, she wasn't certain whether she'd conceived in their circle or on this seat.

Luke climbed in on the driver's side. "I'd offer you a penny for your thoughts, but at today's prices I seriously doubt it would buy a single brain wave."

Bonnie tossed her head, fighting off the sadness which

had been her constant companion for seven years. It was nothing short of miraculous when her tactic worked. "I'll tell you for the price of a cream soda from the nearest vending machine."

"A cream soda, you say?" He pretended serious consideration of her counteroffer. "Fair enough."

True to his word, Luke steered the truck into the gas station on the outskirts of town. Bonnie burst into laughter when he emerged from the vending area imitating a wine steward.

Bearing her opened pop bottle on an overturned oil pan which he had borrowed and covered with a paper towel, he kept her in stitches with a ridiculous running commentary about the soda's clarity and bouquet. As they drove away, laughing hilariously and sharing her pop, the baffled station attendant just scratched his head and returned the oil pan to the service bay.

On the way to Atlanta, Luke told her why he'd built the cluster-housing development that Darlene and Dave were moving into. Bonnie was completely caught up in his enthusiastic explanation and thoroughly impressed by his firm commitment to what he termed the "affordable housing revolution."

"Have I put you to sleep yet?" he asked at one point.

"No," she answered truthfully. "In fact, as one of those millions of renters you were discussing, I find it fascinating." She sighed. "It's crazy, you know. Here I clear more money in one year than my father did in five years combined, yet I still can't afford to purchase a traditional house."

Luke pounded his fist emphatically on the steering wheel. "That's because the costs—land, materials, energy, to name a few—have tripled in the last ten years." He smiled wryly, as if chagrined by the vehement tone of his outburst. "There I go again, spewing out facts and figures like a computer run amok. But housing *is* a basic need of society, and in this country it's almost become a birth-right."

"So you're reconstructing the American dream?" Bon-nie marveled.

"Exactly." He smiled and she could tell that her remark had struck a deeply responsive chord in him. "If the builders and architects won't create affordable alter-natives for the general public," he summarized succinct-ly, "who will?"

They lapsed into a companionable silence then. A little north of Atlanta proper, Luke took an exit off the highway and turned the truck onto a rutted, red-clay road. Judging from the numerous graders, backhoes and other heavy pieces of construction machinery, she as-sumed they were nearing the site of his pet project.

As he adroitly steered the pickup along the bumpy excuse for a road, her gaze strayed to his hands. Strong. Work-roughened. Yet tender. Capable of controlling pas-sion and bestowing pleasure with a gently masterful touch.

"Well, what do you think?" He stopped the truck in front of a long row of completed, two-story structures and turned to her with an expectant expression.

Bonnie never had a chance to respond. "Well, it's about time you two arrived!" Darlene declared as she yanked open the door on the driver's side. "We've been keeping lunch for you nearly a half hour now."

"Hey, Luke!" Dave greeted as he jogged toward the

truck. "Come see what a difference the skylight has made since it was installed."

After exchanging tolerantly amused glances at their siblings' enthusiasm, Bonnie and Luke climbed out of the pickup and followed Darlene and Dave toward their house. While they walked, Bonnie made a point of studying the first finished cluster of homes, easily identifying those exterior features which Luke had discussed with such pride and enthusiasm during their drive from Rebel's Ridge.

Cleverly constructed, the front and back walls of each unit were staggered to insure that next-door neighbors wouldn't invade one another's privacy every time they looked outside. Built of red brick for low maintenance, the eight completed dwellings had uniquely distinguishing touches, thanks to the architect's innovative wrought-iron designs and the painting crew's use of different but complementary colors on doors and wood trim.

In order to reduce land costs there were no front lawns to speak of. From inside the house, however, she saw that the rear picture window overlooked a large backyard which could be shared and maintained by all the residents of a particular cluster.

This project represented so many important things, she realized. A new era in home ownership for millions of people. A lofty goal that Luke had set when he'd had nothing but a hatful of debts and a headful of dreams. A genuine achievement on his part.

"Well, what do you think?" He repeated his original question when he joined her at the window.

"I think it's remarkable," she replied honestly.

He wrapped his arm around her waist in mute gratitude.

"Seeing this," she whispered, "reminds me of an industrious little boy who built a tree house from scrap lumber."

"As I recall, he had a pig-tailed gofer who didn't know a drawshave from a bread knife." He gathered her against his chest, locking his hands around her middle. "I wonder whatever became of those two crazy kids?"

Bonnie felt the tears rolling down her cheeks and was helpless to stop them. Ducking her head, she moved out of his arms and fumbled ineffectually through her purse for a tissue. Luke took a folded handkerchief from his pocket, and she used it to wipe her eyes, removing most of her carefully applied makeup in the process.

"Do I look like a raccoon?" She raised her face to him.

"A little bit from the front." He dropped a kiss on her hair. "But I'd have to see your ringtail to be certain."

"Lunchtime!" Darlene announced cheerfully.

Bonnie repaired her makeup in the bathroom before joining the others.

"This is the best I can do since you need to keep the dining room table at home for the reception." Darlene had set their plates of sandwiches and cookies on tray tables in the living room. "Luke said that he'd move the table for us sometime next week."

Next week. Bonnie fought the threat of more tears. She'd almost forgotten that she was loving on borrowed time. Next week, she'd be back in business making bag lunches for a picnic benefit in Central Park, basting hams and baking biscuits for a museum opening on Fifth

Avenue and eating her heart out for what might have been if she and Luke had only handled their problems more maturely seven years ago.

"What do you think of our Waterford chandelier?" Darlene asked. "Luke ordered it scaled to size so it wouldn't overwhelm the room."

Giving herself a brisk mental shake, Bonnie admired the exquisite fixture hanging like a crystal dewdrop from the ceiling. After they ate, Luke telephoned his office while Darlene and Dave took her on a guided tour of their new home.

The house was compact, yet the ingenious use of mirrors and skylights added the illusion of depth and space. Interior walls were shared, an energy-saving technique, but the architect had made certain that the front and back walls had large windows offering good light exposure and wonderful views of the surrounding landscape.

"Luke claims that traditional homes for the average-income family have disappeared with the quarter hamburger," Dave said when they went upstairs to look around.

In the bathroom, Darlene pointed out the corner which had been reserved for their sunken marble tub. "Luke says that just because we're living efficiently it doesn't mean we can't also live elegantly."

When they came downstairs, Luke was nowhere to be seen inside the house. They went outdoors and found him consulting with his crew over a set of building specifications.

Waiting quietly while he answered the workers' questions and resolved their problems, Bonnie thought of a dozen things she wanted to tell him when they were alone again. Her heart raced at a reckless pace.

"My foreman is going to ride back to the office with us." Luke nodded at the burly, hard-hatted man standing beside him. "We need to talk to the architect about some changes in the blueprints before we begin the next cluster."

What could she say? Hoping her disappointment wasn't blatantly obvious she murmured, "Fine," and rode into Atlanta wedged between two sets of shoulders that made the cab seem terribly cramped for space.

Luke parked his truck in the Dunwoody section of Atlanta where his office was located, then waved his foreman on ahead of them. "This shouldn't take long," he promised, briskly ushering her toward a sleek prismatic tower of polished granite and glass. "Chris knows we're on our way."

After they'd entered the stunning structure, Bonnie read the directory and learned that they were in the lobby of the "Ford Industrial Complex." She couldn't contain an exclamation of pleased surprise. "You own this building!"

He laughed and escorted her into the elevator. "A monument to my *edifice* complex, I suppose."

"From a tree house to a skyscraper," she teased as they were whisked to his penthouse suite. "Now *that's* progress."

When they stepped out of the elevator, it was like a hot wire had shot an electric spark through the office. Word processors ceased production. Conversations stopped in mid-sentence. And every female gaze fixed on the two of them as if drawn by some inexplicable force.

Had they suddenly grown a matching set of horns or something? Bonnie glanced at Luke and started to make light of the devastating effect his mere presence had on his employees. A shadow near the receptionist's desk caught her eye and the joke died on her lips. She didn't notice the floor-to-ceiling windows spilling sunlight onto the plush silver-gray carpeting. She didn't see the imported marble desktops or the suede furniture. Her attention fastened instead on one anguished gray gaze. And with an instinct as old as the ages, Bonnie knew she was looking into the eyes of a woman in love—with Luke.

7

A bolt of jealousy riveted Bonnie to the spot, while a profound despair flooded the other woman's sweet-sad face. Busy rifling through a stack of messages that the receptionist had handed him, Luke stood between them.

"You must be Bonnie." Her low-key voice wavering, the brunette beauty stepped forward. "I'm Chris Miller."

Bonnie recognized her name as the one Darlene had mentioned and felt as if she'd been physically slapped by Luke. What gall! Arranging for an ex-wife to meet a current mistress! Betraying none of the rage boiling up inside her, she replied with cold politeness, "How do you do."

"I'm sorry—I should have introduced you." Luke looked up, his broad smile including both of them. "Chris is the architect who designed the cluster-housing development that you saw today."

Her throat clogged with unspeakable fury, Bonnie didn't trust herself to respond. How convenient for him, having her on the payroll!

"Are the blueprints ready for me to review?" he asked.

"They're on the conference table," Chris answered softly.

"Let's get this done so the crew can break ground on the new cluster tomorrow. It shouldn't take you more than a few minutes to sketch in the changes." Luke glanced at Bonnie. "You're welcome to join the meeting, if you want."

She shook her head, unable yet to deliver a civil reply.

"Make yourself at home in my office, then—first door to your left," he invited before heading in the opposite direction, his mind obviously occupied with altering the blueprints.

Chris Miller smiled sadly, then turned and followed Luke.

The man was totally amoral! Bonnie squeezed her eyes shut, sick to her soul as she relived her other encounter with one of his playmates. Her hands clenched into fists, nails digging cruelly into her palms, as she struggled to suppress a scream of outrage.

"Mrs. Ford?" The receptionist's voice was tinged with concern.

Hearing herself addressed as a married woman after all these years, Bonnie went stiff with shock. What a vulgar situation! No wonder the secretaries had stopped working when she stepped off the elevator with him. Melodrama was infinitely more fascinating than facts and figures.

"Mrs. Ford," the receptionist repeated, "are you—"

"It's *Ms.* Ford," she corrected between clenched teeth, "and I'll be in his office." She retreated to her sanctuary, shut the door and leaned back against the solid wood. But there was no hiding from the truth.

Twice now, she'd let her heart mislead her. And with the same man, no less. *Stupid!* an inner voice taunted. How long she stood there enmeshed in misery, she didn't know. Finally, she walked to the windows overlooking the lush landscape below. *Had Chris designed that, too?* She pressed her forehead to the glass and the other buildings nearby blurred into one gray smudge before her tear-filled eyes.

The gentle tapping at the door reverberated like thunder through the silent room. Bonnie didn't bother answering—it wasn't locked. Nor did she turn around to see who had entered—it didn't matter.

"I'm sorry for the intrusion," Chris Miller began quietly as she moved toward the marble-topped desk in the center of the office, "but we really should talk."

"What's there to talk about?" Bonnie pivoted, her lips curved in a derisive smile. "You must be good with numbers so you know one man isn't divisible by two women."

"Nobody knows that better than . . ." Chris's voice cracked, and she quickly cleared her throat. Her expressive artist's hands trembled slightly as she lifted the lid off the small, loblolly pine box sitting on a corner of the desk. She removed a cigarette and, hesitantly, offered it to Bonnie.

"No, thank you," she refused curtly.

Chris's slender fingers encircled the slim silver lighter that she took from the pocket of her drafting smock. She inhaled deeply, as if the smoke would give her the courage to speak. "I never had any nesting instincts that I can recall. Marriage. Motherhood. It always sounded like a regular Cinderella crock . . ."

"Then you met Luke?" Bonnie prompted cynically.

"In college." Chris's gray gaze focused on the nearest wall.

Bonnie looked in the same direction and immediately noticed the evidence of another accomplishment. Framed and centered among his personal photographs and professional awards hung his engineering degree. Sadness shimmered in Bonnie's amber eyes. Here he'd finished school, and she'd never had an inkling. What else didn't she know about the man who possessed her soul?

"It was the last semester of my graduate program at Georgia Tech," Chris continued slowly. "Luke had enrolled in order to complete his engineering credits, and we had some classes together—most of them related to environmental design and energy conservation techniques in the construction field."

Chris paused, puffing nervously on her cigarette, then shrugged her shoulders. "Coffee after class. Late-hour study sessions at the library during finals week. He'd just started his own company, and I needed a job after graduation." Her voice thickened with emotion. "Our professional goals were so similar that I was fool enough to begin fantasizing—"

"I don't want to hear this—this saga of your affair with Luke," Bonnie interrupted, her tone defensive.

"You *need* to hear it," Chris insisted, extinguishing her

cigarette with sharp stabs in the heavy glass ashtray. "You need to know the truth."

"Why?" Bonnie demanded vehemently.

"Because . . ." Chris's words were strangled in a heartbroken sob as her brittle control snapped under the stress.

Bonnie reacted instinctively, hurrying around the corner of the desk to embrace the desolate young woman. She desperately wanted to hate Chris Miller. Yet their shared sorrow prevailed over her wounded pride. Hadn't she also shed similarly tortured tears because of this man?

"You were the ghost who slept between us in his bed," Chris accused brokenly. "When he reached for me in the middle of the night, he was really reaching for you. I knew it from the beginning but . . ."

Bonnie held her close and let her cry, understanding completely. Chris eventually composed herself and moved out of Bonnie's arms, putting some necessary distance between them. "He was so tender, such an incredible—" She broke off, her sigh laced with sadness. "But you already know that." She lowered her head, her hair falling like a dark velvet curtain across her fragile face. "He hasn't touched me since the day that Darlene announced you were coming home for the wedding."

Bonnie swallowed the apology that had automatically come to mind. Old habits died hard. But she *wasn't* sorry and damned if she'd say she was! When she finally spoke, her voice was husky with hurt. "You'll have him back Sunday night—hopefully none the worse for the wear."

"I've submitted my resignation," Chris murmured. "It's effective Monday morning."

A twinge of relief sputtered through Bonnie before shame smothered it. If both of them left, Luke would be alone. "Where will you go?"

"Houston. I've been accepted as a junior member of a major firm there. They are setting some very exciting design trends in the industry. When I sent slides of our various projects with my letter of application, they said my work shows promise."

"From what I saw today, they're right," Bonnie offered graciously.

Chris smiled wryly. "As the architect of my own disaster, the least I can do is salvage what's left and build something decent from it."

"Luke will miss you, I'm sure." Bonnie was surprised to realize how sincerely she meant that.

"He's already forgotten that I exist, except in a professional sense," Chris rebutted softly. She squared her shoulders. "Thank you—for listening and for letting me love him."

Before Bonnie could reply, the heavy door swung open and Luke entered the office.

"If I'm interrupting an important discussion, point me in another direction." He crossed the room and stopped beside Bonnie, waving the typewritten pages and addressed envelopes that he held. "But if this is strictly a gab session, you're the ones who will have to relocate. These bids are begging to be signed, sealed and delivered."

Chris gazed at him, her somber gray eyes an eloquent study in grief. "I was just leaving."

"Good-bye, Chris." It was the first time that Bonnie had said her name aloud. It would also be the last time. "Good luck."

One bruised but unbeaten angel made her exit.

One woman remained, standing by her man for a little while.

"This doesn't *remotely* resemble a shopping center!"

"I never said it did."

"You *promised* that you'd take me to the grocery store."

"But I never said when."

Bonnie and Luke sat in the cab of his pickup. He'd parked atop a grassy knoll overlooking a cup-shaped hollow filled with redbuds, dogwoods and other trees in full bloom. Towering pines spired from the center of the dale while the late afternoon sun hung like a goldpiece over the horizon, baking the countryside in its quiet heat.

After a dozen legitimate delays, they'd finally left his office. She'd thought they were going grocery shopping, then returning to Rebel's Ridge for dinner. Obviously a mistaken assumption on her part since, instead, he'd driven straight to this beautiful but virtually deserted area on the far eastern edge of Atlanta.

She eyed him suspiciously when he slid his arm around her shoulders and drew her closer to his hard frame. "Am I being waylaid, by any chance?"

"Do you really want me to answer that?" His hand grazed her breast, not entirely by accident judging from the devilish grin deepening his dimples.

"I think you just did." Curling her slim, bare legs beneath her, Bonnie nestled contentedly against Luke, marveling anew at the exquisite physical fit that always left her feeling a little delirious. His breathing was steady, regular; he was completely relaxed and she hated to make waves.

What possible difference could a couple of stolen hours make in the scheme of an entire week? It was all they had—much more than she'd expected, yet not nearly enough. Surely, somewhere in Dixie's sprawling, sophisticated capital there were fully stocked supermarkets that kept late hours. Weren't there? Just to be on the safe side, she raised her head to ask him.

His eyes were closed, and she could almost count the individual dark lashes lying against his prominent, sun-bronzed cheekbones. In repose, his face lost none of its vitality but gained a slight measure of vulnerability.

She shifted her position carefully so as not to disturb him, then studied him in sleep. How and when had he gotten that tiny white scar which extended the cleft under his chin? The cab grew warmer as the day neared dusk, and she wondered who'd shaped the sideburns waving damply around his ears. Did he ever remember those horribly uneven trims she used to give him when they were too poor to pay the price of a decent haircut?

Bonnie rested her head against his chest, her sigh tinged with untold regrets. If she hadn't become pregnant, would they have married anyway? Or would they have drifted apart and found other partners, as childhood sweethearts often do? These were questions without answers, yet she couldn't picture herself with anyone else but Luke.

His arm tightened around her shoulder, and she knew that he'd awakened. When she reached up and touched his hand, their fingers entwined as securely as moonflower vines taking hold in spring. A woodpecker *thunked* on a dead elm somewhere off in the distance while, nearby, the peepers sang sharp and ceaselessly.

"It's peaceful around here this time of day," he said. "Why don't we stretch our legs a bit?"

"I'd like that," she agreed softly, tucking her purse under the seat.

They both climbed out on the driver's side, and Luke locked the doors. As far as she could see, no power lines or billboards spoiled the natural beauty of the surroundings. Holding hands, they started down the gentle slope, leaving the sun's last hot light as Bonnie followed his sure-footed lead along a path canopied by the trees.

She ducked under a swaying gourd, scooped out and hanging by a thin wire from a sycamore branch—home for some fortunate family of purple martins. "Do you come here often?"

"Whenever life starts going its own way instead of my way," he admitted as they left the shelter of the woods and walked across a clearing toward a narrow creek. He crouched beside the stream, took out his pocketknife and cut a sprig of new watercress from a clump growing in the clear rill. When he stood, he put away the knife, tucked the greens into his shirt pocket, then shrugged. "Whenever my dreams start drying up."

Bonnie went to him, alarmed by the note of defeat she heard in his normally vigorous voice. Had something bad happened at the office? There had been so many phone calls and conferences—maybe he'd lost an important bid to a competitor.

Confused, uncertain of how best to comfort him

because she didn't know the actual source of his despair, she reached out and smoothed his breeze-tousled hair off his brow.

Luke caught her wrist and brought her palm to his mouth. His tongue leisurely traced each line before boldly invading the space between her fingers. "Don't leave me, Bonnie," he murmured roughly against her tingling skin. "Stay and let me love you."

"I'm here," she asserted, answering only for the moment. Her breath quickened when their bodies came together. "I'm here, Luke."

A gentle wind whispered through the pines. They linked hands, four becoming two. They kissed, two becoming one. A division of love. Strengthening them both. Wreaking havoc with her senses.

She tasted the honeyed demand of his tongue and felt the urgent strain of his need. Yet he didn't hurry. Lowering his head, he savored the satiny curve of her neck. First one side. Then the other. She shuddered, her knees weak with wanting, as he fed her desire with his hungry mouth.

The cicadas chirped anxiously, echoing her heartbeat. And still, he didn't hurry. Reclaiming her parted lips he slowly sipped of her sweetness, then gradually drew her tongue into an erotic duel. When he freed her hands, she slipped them beneath his cotton shirt and her fingers trailed along the hard length of his spine. Hooking his thumbs under the straps of her sundress he slid them off her shoulders and exposed, for his eyes only, her softly scented flesh, aching now for his soothing caress.

Scuttling pinecones seized his attention. Glancing toward the stand of trees across the gurgling brook, Luke smiled. "We have company."

"Oh, no," she groaned. Imagining the worst— innocent children or giggling teenagers—Bonnie huddled shamefaced against his shirt front. "Do something," she whispered frantically. "Chase them away."

"Be still," he warned quietly. "They're crossing over."

Listening to the footsteps splashing in the stream, she could hardly breathe. He chuckled and she cringed. Had he forgotten that she was standing there bare-breasted, for heaven's sake? She squirmed, reminding him of her embarrassing predicament, and he curved her closer to his body.

"Very slowly now, turn your head," he murmured.

Timidly, she complied and peeked sideways. A wisp of relieved laughter escaped her throat when she saw the white-tailed doe and her spotted fawn munching clover near the edge of the clearing.

"We're trespassing," he said. "Let's go."

Moving cautiously so as not to frighten the feeding deer, they backed out of the clearing. The doe raised her head once, her unblinking brown eyes watching their retreat through the twilight.

Luke kissed the tip of Bonnie's nose, smiled and slipped the straps of her sundress up onto her shoulders. Gazing wistfully at the rugged set of his features, she felt a twinge of disappointment at the thought of returning to the real world so soon. As if he'd read her mind, he steered her away from the path leading up to the road.

"Where are we going?" she asked.

"Where I should have taken you in the first place."

The cabin sat in the middle of a second, smaller clearing.

"Another monument to your edifice complex?" she teased.

"To tell the truth, I bought the hollow with the intention of clearing it for my cluster development." He held her hand as they neared the log house. "But the abstract showed that this place was a nineteenth-century coach stop. It gave me such a sense of history, I just couldn't bring myself to destroy it." He grinned ruefully. "You're not the only one with an overactive conscience."

"It tilts!" Bonnie exclaimed, eyeing the support lintel above the front door and the sloping planked floors inside.

"There's a list to it," Luke agreed as he lit a candle and placed it in a brass holder. "It's not likely to fall down around us tonight, though."

While sparsely furnished, the one-room cabin was quite cozy. The two windows were clean, and the neatly hemmed canvas curtains he'd hung over the bottom panes insured their privacy. He had used a concrete mixture to replace the original rock and mud chinking in the dovetailed walls, which gave off a wonderful old timber aroma.

"No electricity?" Bonnie kicked off her sandals.

"Not a volt." Luke set the candleholder on the oak chest.

"No running water?" She shrugged out of her sundress.

"Not a drop." He pulled his shirt off over his head.

"No telephone?" Her half-slip and bikini panties fell in a satin pool around her bare feet.

"You're the only one I'm talking to tonight." His jeans and shorts landed in a heap atop his abandoned loafers.

"How perfectly authentic." She folded back the bear paw patterned quilt before climbing into the four-poster rope bed. "But tell me, aren't you violating your builders' sacred oath, 'the whole planet is a potential shopping center,' by restoring this place?"

"No." The candle flame flickered with his approach.

"Well, then," she breathed eagerly, holding out her arms to him, "I suppose you'll simply have to violate me instead."

"You must have read my mind." He paused beside the bed.

"No." She forced herself to look him straight in the eye. "Let's just say that your intentions are pretty conspicuous at this moment."

"Now that we know you've got twenty-twenty vision," he said huskily, "we'll have to see how the rest of you measures up."

Luke lay down, and the clean fragrance of fresh straw wafted up around them as they sank back together into the soft ticking. Bonnie melted like warm, wild honey under his feverish caresses and the deep, loving strokes of his tongue. Her fingers teased him and her lips tasted him as she made her own survey, memorizing each muscle.

Thighs and arms interlocked as their mouths savored what they might never sample again so completely. When he moved up over her, she cupped the solid curve of his buttocks and marveled at the smooth ripple of sinew beneath her hands. Their heartbeats set the rhythm and their bodies kept perfect pace.

Primitive shadows danced on the ancient walls while the candlelight cast a mellow glow over their entwining limbs, illuminating the physical evidence of a spiritual bond that neither time nor law had truly dissolved. The taper burned low first, and the world slumbered, unaware that the word *forever* could mean hours in love's unlimited vocabulary.

"Luke?" She shook him gently. "Luke!"

"Mmm?" His answer was muffled in the crook of her neck.

"Are you asleep?" She shifted her position slightly.

"Not anymore."

"I'm starved!" she whispered urgently.

"You're insatiable," he growled dreamily.

Bonnie's stomach rumbled. "I haven't had a bite of food since we ate lunch with Darlene and Dave."

He raised his head and smiled mischievously. "Oh, you mean *that* appetite?"

"Yes, *that* appetite." She swatted his hand when it wandered with warm abandon, slower and lower over her stomach. "I'm hungry."

"Me, too," he murmured as his mouth made a delicious descent and nibbled ravenously from the offering of her lips.

The flavor and texture of his kiss made her forget the reason that she'd awakened. But her stomach's second, noisy protest during the romantic delay reminded them both of her original purpose in rousing him. It took some rather ingenious untangling of legs and arms before they were free to search the single cupboard, bare but for a tin of beef stew and a bottle of lemon-lime soda.

"Tell me, Father Hubbard," she teased, "do you entertain all of your overnight guests this lavishly, or am I one of the privileged few?"

Luke set the manual can opener aside and turned to her, tipping her chin to meet his serious expression. "I've never had another woman in this cabin, Bonnie. I never will."

She knew in that moonlit moment that he spoke the truth and felt giddy with relief. He embraced her and their mouths fused, sealing off that part of their past and healing another of envy's old wounds. She could face the future now, not having to envision him sharing this special place with a stranger.

"Sorry." Bonnie ducked her head, embarrassed when her stomach growled impatiently again. "I'd muzzle it if I could."

He released her and grinned. "Now that I'm up and about, food is beginning to sound like a pretty good idea to me, too."

She took the one spoon and he used the one fork in the cabin. They sprinkled the wilting watercress that he'd cut earlier over the cold, canned stew and sipped the tepid soda straight from the bottle. She couldn't remember a meal she'd ever enjoyed so much.

When they were finished eating, he raced her to the creek, where they washed their utensils and rinsed off their hands. She didn't really plan on pushing him in. But he made such a nice splash when she did.

Bellowing like some crazed monster from the deep, he rose out of the stream and carried her, kicking and squealing, into the waist-high water. Sloshing and dunking each other, they excited a riot of raucous scolding from every bird guarding a nest in the trees.

As she'd saved herself for him these seven years, so had Bonnie saved her laughter. It bubbled merrily inside her now and pealed from her throat, joining Luke's hearty roar in a jubilant chorus of midnight delight. Weak with hilarity they clung to one another as they stumbled out of the water, gasping for air.

Sprawling side by side on the mossy bank, neither of them noticed the stars winking brightly above them. Nor did they see the moonlight spilling in silvery streams from the sky. Their eyes mirrored only each other, and their silliness gave way to seriousness as their two minds knew but a single thought.

"I love you." Their voices coupled, husky and soft.

Luke rolled onto his back and Bonnie straddled him with her knees. Slowly, thoroughly, she kissed each sinewed inch of him. His fingers toyed with her wet hair as she drove him near the exquisite edge of no return. Regaining control with a harsh growl he pulled her upward and mouthed her dusky rose nipples, which blossomed under the tender torture of his tongue.

When he finally fit her onto him, she received several strong thrusts before gentling him beneath her. Again she tested his endurance until finally he secured her hips with his hands and drove upward, leaving her breathless with ecstasy. Her body closed around him as their sighs mingled with the night mist.

"Why did you say yesterday that you wished you'd made me pregnant again?"

Smoke spiraled from the glowing red tip of Luke's

cigarette toward the beamed ceiling of the cabin. "To make amends, I suppose."

"Amends?" Bonnie sat up and hugged her knees, moving for the first time since he'd carried her inside and put her on the bed. "For what?"

"Hey, I thought that you'd already accepted my plea of temporary insanity on this issue." Because his grave tone belied his teasing remark, she waited quietly until he continued. "You wanted our other baby so much . . ."

Fear clawed at her throat but she found the courage to ask, "And you didn't?"

"I wanted *you*, Bonnie. If that meant having the baby, too . . ." He shrugged. "Remember, I thought with my glands instead of my brains in those days."

She rested her cheek on her kneecaps, hurt by his honesty but relieved to hear the truth at long last. "Then you didn't blame me when I miscarried?"

"Hell, no," he admitted hoarsely. "In fact, I blamed myself."

"Why?" She looked over her shoulder in surprise.

He crushed his cigarette in the ashtray, then pressed his head back into the pillow. "Because for several years afterwards, I believed that I was the cause of it."

"Whatever gave you that idea?" she whispered incredulously.

"You probably don't recall, but we'd made some pretty passionate love the night before it happened." He pulled her down and she laid her head on his chest. "While you were in the recovery room, the doctor asked me if you had engaged in any *strenuous* activity that might have brought on an early labor." His voice vibrated with the pain of remembrance. "It was like he had pointed his finger straight at me. I just knew that if I'd kept my hands off you—"

"And I thought you were mad at me when I came home from the hospital," she murmured. "We'd quit talking and stopped touching—"

"I felt so guilty that I could hardly look you in the eye, much less take you in my arms. Whenever I heard you crying, I died a little inside." His heavy sigh stirred her hair. "After I lost my job, I went crazy trying to prove I was still a man. By the time I came to my senses, you were gone—living in another world entirely."

It was history now. But was it a lesson learned too late? Bonnie raised herself up, her tears raining softly on his face while Luke held her through that darkest hour. And a passion born of friendship, fostered in sorrow, finally came of age.

8

Morning dawned much too early. They had to leave; it wasn't a matter of choice. After washing up in the clear creek water they dressed in rumpled clothes that they'd forgotten to hang up the night before, then stripped the bed they'd shared. Bonnie's heart weighed heavily when Luke locked up the cabin, and her legs felt leaden as they climbed the hill toward the spot where he'd parked the truck.

He suggested that they stop somewhere for breakfast since the grocery store wouldn't open for another hour, and she nodded in weary agreement. She wasn't hungry, but even fools need their nourishment. Besides, a strong cup of coffee might stimulate her brain cells. Lord knew they needed any boost they could get.

They ate in silence, exchanging only brief glances

across the formica table of the cramped pancake house. Under ordinary circumstances, she would have demolished the buckwheat stack dripping fresh-churned butter and sweet maple syrup. Now, the few bites she managed were simply a means of gaining strength to get through the day. When their half-empty plates were cleared and their cups refilled, he lit a cigarette, and she made a great production of stirring sugar into her coffee.

"I lied to you last night," Luke admitted levelly. "When I said I wished I'd gotten you pregnant to make amends," he explained as she tipped her head in curiosity. "The truth is, I figured it would give us the perfect excuse to try again."

Shocked, she felt her gaze widen with incredulity. *"What?"*

He shrugged. "Long-distance love and a weekend marriage—I realize it's not exactly the romantic ideal. But it *is* an alternative, hopefully a temporary one, for people like us with careers in different cities."

She searched his face for humor as the import of his words made an impact on her. When she spoke, it was barely a squeak. "Is that a *proposal?*"

He broke into a rueful grin. "And a poorly worded one, at that."

Bonnie set her spoon aside and said the first thing that popped into her head. "But my weekends are usually booked solid. Receptions. Graduations. Conventions." She sighed dismally, knowing she wasn't phrasing this well at all. "It's a good fifty percent of my business. . . ."

"Damn it, then, *you* think of a solution." His dark eyes bored straight through her as he leaned across the table. "I love you—"

"I love you, too," she interrupted hoarsely. "But everything is happening so fast. With Darlene's wedding scheduled in forty-eight hours and all the work yet to be done, can you honestly expect me to make such an important decision in such a short amount of time?"

"I'm not a patient man, Bonnie." Luke leaned back in his chair and folded his hands on the table, his knuckles whitening where they interlaced. "It's certainly not something that I'm proud of—it's just a fact."

"Patience isn't one of my virtues, either." She reached over and laid her hands on his. Feeling his tension, she realized what it had cost him to admit his fault. And she loved him for it.

"Both of us have paid in spades for that vice," he continued slowly. "And while my idea that we remarry might *sound* impetuous, it's all I've been able to think about since you came back."

"I—I don't know. It's so sudden . . . for me, at least." She thought she might drown in the inky depths of his eyes and dropped her gaze. "I need time, Luke . . . to adjust—"

"We've already wasted seven years," he interrupted. "For God's sake, don't squander the rest of our lives as well."

She pulled her hands away, and they sat silently while the waitress totaled their bill. Luke finished his cigarette before he paid the check, and Bonnie used the rest room. She looked into the mirror above the sink and admitted to a special glow she hadn't seen in her face since leaving home.

Home. She closed her eyes while images danced through her mind. If home were truly where the heart resided, then her place was with Luke. But . . . remarriage?

Bonnie crumpled up the paper towel she was using and tossed it into the wastebasket. They clicked in all the right areas, more now than ever before. But having finally opened the lines of communication, could they keep them free—

Someone jiggled the doorknob rather impatiently. Bonnie relinquished the rest room and joined Luke in the pickup. They cruised into Atlanta, each lost in private thought. When he steered into a parking lot and stopped, she peered out the window and realized they were sitting in the shadow of his skyscraper. Just remembering the events of the previous day, she felt her heart plummeting through the floorboards.

"While you're in your office," she murmured, pleating her skirt between her slender fingers, "I'll wait out here."

"I'm only exchanging my truck for my car. I keep one or the other parked here all the time." He got out of the pickup and came around to the passenger side. Her relief must have been evident in her expression because, after he opened the door, a look of keen perception flickered in his eyes. "Look, about Chris—"

"I understand," Bonnie replied calmly. But she couldn't hide the hurt in her voice. "You needed each other, professionally and personally. But that doesn't make it any easier for me." Pivoting, she started across the asphalt lot. "Which one of these belongs to you?"

He grabbed her elbow and spun her around. "You're *not* running out on me this time. If you're upset, let's have it—right here, right now."

For a second she simply stared at him. When she finally spoke, her voice wavered dangerously. "Logically, what you did makes more sense than what I did . . ."

"But?" he prompted, releasing her elbow.

Bitter tears stung her eyes and she bowed her head. "But I *waited* for you, Luke—I realize that now. And you . . . you didn't—"

With an anguished groan, he took her in his arms. "If I'd known—hell, why do you think I let Darlene rattle on about you all the time? She was my only source of information." He buried his face in her hair. "It was torture, listening to her talk. If she said, 'Bonnie saw a Broadway play last night,' I'd immediately wonder who you went with and what you did after the curtain came down."

She stiffened with hurt. "You assumed I was sleeping around and retaliated by doing the same?"

"I assumed you were probably making love with someone, yes. And maybe, subconsciously, I *was* retaliating. Dumb but true," he rasped. "Whenever I pictured you with another man—"

"At least you didn't have a tangible image to contend with," she countered softly. "How do you think I felt after seeing you with that redhead at the Hickory?" She struggled out of his embrace. "How do you think I feel right this minute, knowing your latest ex-lover is working thirty stories above us?"

"Angry, and justifiably so." He tipped his head to one side, his gaze glittering hopefully. "Forgiving?"

She glanced away, nibbling on her lower lip. Forgiving? Like her, wasn't he only human? Hadn't he, too, done what he thought necessary in order to survive?

They'd gone overboard in opposite directions after their divorce. Trying to forget and failing miserably. She looked at him and whispered, "Yes."

They reached out, linking hands, and he led her to his car.

"A Corvette!" She laughed and settled into the low-slung seat on the passenger side. "Talk about going from the ridiculous to the sublime."

"It's got some *wow power*," he admitted with a grin, fastening his safety belt and gesturing for her to follow his example. "I rarely drive it, but I promised Dave and Darlene that they could borrow it after the reception. They're spending Saturday night in the bridal suite at the Peachtree here in Atlanta, then catching a plane Sunday morning for Nassau."

Bonnie froze. She was scheduled to leave Sunday, too. Bending her head, she fumbled with her seat belt.

Luke laid his hands over hers, stilling her clumsy fingers. "We're going to work something out before you go—I swear it."

"How?" She shook her head disbelievingly. "I don't have a free day through June, and July is shaping up almost the same way."

"Damn." He scowled. "If I'm awarded the contract on the shopping center bid that I submitted yesterday—and it's practically a cinch that I will be—we'd break ground in August."

"See?" she insisted dejectedly.

He hit the steering wheel with the heel of his hand. "I'll withdraw the bid, you'll refuse any parties, and August is ours to spend how and where we choose." He shrugged when she sighed. "Look, if we want to be together, we have to make some professional concessions. Design our own future, so to speak."

She frowned. "But a jet-set relationship—"

"Marriage," he corrected firmly. "I won't settle for anything less."

"Don't you think you're rushing things?" she asked weakly, repeating her earlier argument.

"No," he refuted. "I'm just obviously more willing to rack my brain for a solution and make the necessary sacrifices—"

"That's not true," she protested. The old doubts darted about inside her and she felt helpless to combat the attack. "If I honestly believed—"

"You don't trust me," he accused flatly.

Her gaze clung to him, silently pleading for empathy. So many adjustments and so little time!

"I guess I can't really blame you." Luke's mouth slanted in a self-mocking smile as he inserted the key into the ignition. "Hell, everybody knows that a skunk can't change its stripes. Right?"

Bonnie started to deny that and explain her hesitation more fully, but the roaring motor drowned out her words. Expecting a wild ride to the grocery store she braced herself against the plush leather seat, yet he handled the sports car as carefully as a Sunday driver.

Inside the supermarket he pushed the cart while she squeezed, sniffed and snapped before selecting the finest produce and fruit. His attitude proved a pleasant surprise since shopping had been his least favorite chore during their marriage. He even knew the butcher by name, which helped considerably when she rejected the briskets already displayed and requested special cuts.

Although she considered the preparation of food an art and could easily spend as many hours in the grocery aisles as collectors did in galleries, she stuck strictly to her list so as not to strain his endurance.

At the cash register, the cute blond clerk checked Luke out more thoroughly than she did the contents of the cart. Bonnie corrected the errors she caught, bit back the reprimand she was longing to make and scrawled her name on the traveler's checks she took from her purse. That he neither encouraged the clerk's flirtations nor responded to them did nothing to tame the green-eyed monster stirring inside her.

Bonnie realized that her unfounded reaction smacked of paranoia. Luke didn't exist exclusively to please her. He was a person entitled to his independence, not a possession. In her heart, though, she was still terrified. A healthy relationship required mutual trust. And since time hadn't remedied her fears, she had to wonder whether her condition was incurable where Luke was concerned. If so, any commitment she made now would be less than sound in a future crisis.

She remained withdrawn during their drive to Rebel's Ridge, and he made no attempt to distract her with small talk. Their silence was more reflective than sultry, because the issue between them was too serious to trivialize and too important to ignore.

"Hey, Luke!" Dave bustled out of the house when they'd parked in the driveway. "I promised Darlene that

I'd mow the meadow today, but the tractor won't start."
He grabbed two sacks of groceries out of the car and
carried them up the porch steps. "Can you give me a
hand when you're free?"

"Sure thing." Luke unloaded two more brown bags.

Bonnie experienced a brief twinge of worry about how
Darlene would view her overnight absence, then
squelched it and followed the men inside. She wasn't
ashamed of loving Luke and refused to hang her head or
apologize.

"Oh, good, you bought brisket!" Darlene had already
emptied two sacks and was busy unpacking a third when
Bonnie entered the kitchen. "Are you going to smother it
with onions and make gravy?"

"The bride had onion breath," Luke teased. "I can
already hear the gossip sizzling along the grapevine."

"The groom has a choice—eat them with me or weep
alone." Darlene tossed Dave a Bermuda onion, then
cheered boisterously when he pretended to take a big
bite out of it.

The horseplay continued until Bonnie issued her ulti-
matum. "I'm going to run upstairs and shower. If the rest
of you dear folks aren't productively occupied when I'm
through, I'll start assigning chores."

Silence reigned supreme when she returned to the
kitchen dressed for work. She'd shampooed her hair and
wound it into a gleaming topknot so it wouldn't keep
falling across her face. Her legs and arms were bare
because of the shorts and sleeveless shirt she wore.
Thanks to the lack of air conditioning and the full blast of
the oven, the afternoon promised to be a hot one.

Efficient by nature and a whiz with the whisk, Bonnie had her chocolate cake stirred and baking in record time. When the layers were cooled, she would cover them with foil and let them season a day before frosting them with fudge and decorating the sinfully sweet concoction with spun-sugar flowers. Whistling an off-key rendition of the wedding march, she whipped up a tangy beer marinade for the briskets and a rich basil dressing for the pesto salad she planned to serve during the buffet-style reception.

Bonnie found it nothing short of amazing that she felt so energetic after her virtually sleepless night. Looking out the window, she saw Dave riding the mower around the meadow and Darlene pinning freshly washed sheets to the clothesline. She smiled, picturing Luke snoozing in the shade of a tree somewhere. Maybe when she finished in here, she'd sneak out and curl up beside him for a while.

The idea quickened both her pulse and the pace of her clean-up. She loved him. She always had and always would. But now that she'd had an opportunity to mull their situation over, she needed to share her thoughts with him.

Given their volatile temperaments, could they really live together again—even on a part-time basis? And what kind of marriage would they have, anyway? Flying back and forth across the country. Discussing personal problems and professional triumphs over the telephone. And suppose they decided eventually to have children? After her difficult experience with pregnancy, she definitely didn't want to be alone—

"It smells heavenly in here!" Darlene came through the back door, an empty clothes basket in hand. "If you need a taste tester, I'm available."

Bonnie slapped her sister's fingers when they strayed too close to the cooling cake layers. "If you're looking for something to do, dry those mixing bowls and pans in the drainer and put them away."

"Sorry, I'm busy dismantling a waist-high laundry sculpture." Darlene opened the basement door. "By the way, do you remember Mrs. Painter, the widow down the road?"

"Of course." Even after all these years, Bonnie still had a soft spot for the grandmotherly woman who'd always had a stick of gum and a sympathetic ear to spare for the children in town. "Why do you ask?"

"Well, she called this morning and asked if she could drop by tomorrow around noon."

"I hope you told her yes."

Darlene nodded and started downstairs.

"What's Luke up to?" Bonnie asked in a casual tone.

"He went fishing," Darlene replied over her shoulder.

"Fishing!" Bonnie almost dropped the bowl she was drying.

Darlene stopped and turned around. "After you threatened all of us, he helped Dave start the mower, said 'What could be more productive than catching our dinner' and left." She grinned. "He also reminded us that there's a package of hot dogs in the freezer. Just in case."

Fishing! Bonnie couldn't argue with his logic because she hadn't planned a thing for dinner, but the rest of the afternoon stretched out long and lonely ahead of her. It didn't take two people to operate the washing machine, and Darlene had already swept the carpet and dusted what little furniture remained in the house. Dave was done with the meadow and noisily mowing the yard.

Maybe she'd give Sueanne a call. She'd never seen her house or met her children. And she really did need to talk with someone.

Sueanne answered on the eleventh ring, her voice breathless and her words rushed. "Oh, I'd love to visit with you, but I've got a doctor's appointment and I'm running late." She laughed wryly. "Jon, my oldest, decided to fingerpaint with raw eggs on the kitchen floor. And Vicki added coffee grounds for color."

The phone on Sueanne's end clattered loudly then as she dropped it. Bonnie heard two swats, immediately followed by a chorus of wails. The miniature monsters were getting their just desserts from the sound of it. A few seconds later, the sound of crooning hushed the anguished cries of childhood.

"Sorry about that," Sueanne said contritely into the receiver. "I spanked them for picking the three tulips that the dog hadn't trampled. Then they told me they'd brought me flowers because I'm the 'bestest' mommy in the whole world." She sighed, sounding positively exhausted. "I can't win for losing today. Thank heavens Tom is bringing pizza home for dinner. With my luck, anything I cooked would probably turn to cinders before it reached the table."

"I'll let you go, then." Whether in sympathy for her friend or from lack of sleep, Bonnie suddenly felt weary to the bone. "Will I see you at the wedding on Saturday?"

"If I can get organized, you'll see me tonight at the softball game." A thump and a yelp in the background prompted a hasty good-bye from Sueanne.

Bonnie hung up and yawned. For such a small town, people sure stayed busy. She sealed the cake layers with foil and set them on a pantry shelf, done for the day. In the silence, she could almost hear the echo of her own heartbeat. She watched from the kitchen window as Darlene and Dave strolled hand-in-hand across the newly mowed meadow, walking toward the waterfall. The clothes hanging on the line swayed in a soft breeze, drying naturally.

Her sister had a fiancé; her friend had a husband and children; nearly all of her New York acquaintances had similar relationships. She sighed, feeling terribly alone. Everybody had somebody, it seemed.

Too tired to think, she turned and started upstairs. A nap might improve her gloomy outlook. Unaccustomed to sleeping during the day, she found it difficult at first to relax. Gradually, though, she drifted off. Her dreams were filled with pint-sized versions of Luke, a planeload of them, all flying away from her. Tears trickled from beneath her closed lids, falling on her pillow.

The sun's last rays slanted warmly through the window when Bonnie left her bedroom, and the sweet smell of cornbread beckoned from the kitchen.

"Darn! You spoiled our surprise." Despite her grumbling, Darlene smiled as she turned a nicely browned loaf of pone out of the pan and onto a wire rack. "We wanted to have the table set and the food hot before we woke you."

"Look at that nice mess of catfish that Luke caught." Dave finished folding the paper napkins and started sliding them under the silverware arranged beside the dinner plates. "I just hope he left some for the rest of us who enjoy wetting a line."

"By the time you're through honeymooning, little brother," Luke scoffed, "those fingerlings I threw back will be keeper size." His hair waved damply from a shower, and his cheeks were ruddy. He winked broadly when Bonnie joined him at the counter. "Do you want to bet those babies will be full-fledged granddaddies by then?"

"What kind of odds are you giving?" she teased, her voice husky from sleep.

"For you?" He looked into her eyes, and everything else vanished from her sight. "Only the best."

Bonnie tore her gaze away and watched him take the filets from the cornmeal batter and drop them, crackling, into the hot electric skillet. She couldn't concentrate standing this close to him, so she moved a step away. "How can I help?"

"By staying out of our way," Darlene answered firmly. She poured sun tea from a pitcher into a glass full of ice, stirred some freshly cut mint into it, then ordered sternly, "Sit down and drink this."

"But I feel like a three-toed sloth just sitting here," Bonnie protested. "At least let me put the pans to soak or—"

"No." Darlene removed a relish tray from the refrigerator and placed it in the center of the table. "We all decided this might be our last chance to pamper you for a while, and we're going to do it in style. Right, guys?"

"Right!" they agreed together.

Darlene shook her finger under Bonnie's nose. "Now, I'm going out to open the garage doors so Dave can put the mower away. You're not to move a muscle except to lift your glass. Understand?"

"Yes, ma'am," Bonnie replied with mock meekness.

The back door banged shut behind Darlene and Dave.

"Since you're in a yes mood this evening . . ." Luke's suggestion trailed off on a distinctly expectant note.

She tilted her head and said in a teasing tone, "You haven't *asked* me anything yet."

"This morning I asked you to marry me," he reminded her.

"No, you didn't. You *told* me."

"Same difference," he countered evenly, slipping the spatula under the filets and flipping them over, golden side up in the skillet.

"It is not," she argued. "In the restaurant, you presented our life plan already mapped out. And when I didn't immediately agree to your terms—"

"I asked you to think of a solution, and you hightailed it into the rest room," he said laughingly.

"I went to the rest room as a matter of necessity," she corrected with mock indignation.

"I can see I'm not going to get any admissions out of you tonight," Luke grumbled as he scooped the crispy, fried catfish onto a platter. The back door swung open then as Darlene and Dave came inside, and dinner was served.

Bonnie polished off two helpings of everything. Despite the confused thoughts tumbling through her mind, she found herself laughing and joking with the others, relaxed on a full stomach.

"Dave is washing, and I'm drying," Darlene announced as she cleared the plates and utensils from the table. "You two go on outside and sit a spell before the game begins."

A group had already gathered in the meadow, measuring off the distance between the bases and securing the bags in the ground. Someone spotted Luke when he and Bonnie stepped onto the back porch and yelled for him to come help choose the teams so the hitting and pitching strengths would be evenly divided.

He waved his assurance that he'd be there shortly, lit a cigarette and leaned against the door frame. "If I *had* asked you to marry me, how would you have answered?"

"I don't know," she replied honestly. When his eyebrow shot up in surprise, she quickly clarified. "I love you, make no mistake about that. And while I applaud the fact that marriage is going *modern* to accommodate different careers and lifestyles, *I'm* just old-fashioned enough—"

"Hey, Luke!" Tom rounded the corner of the house, his arm draped around Sueanne's shoulders. "Hi, Bonnie!"

Bedlam erupted when the two strawberry-blond children tagging along behind them squealed "Unca' Luke!" in unison and clambered up the porch steps. He crushed out his cigarette, welcomed the toddlers with open arms and swung them both high into the air.

"I'll go inside and relieve Dave as dishwasher," Bonnie offered.

"Aren't you going to play softball?" Tom questioned.

"You fill my position," Sueanne insisted. "I'm out of the line-up until after I deliver. Doctor's orders."

"But I haven't touched a bat in seven years," Bonnie admitted. "I'd be more of a hindrance than a help."

"Good," Luke declared, a devilish gleam in his dark eyes. "We'll put you on Tom's team."

The children squirmed free and dashed down the porch steps. Sueanne lumbered after them, sternly warning them not to touch the pretty flowers.

"Play ball or forfeit the game!" Whoever hurled the dare from the meadow knew exactly how to elicit a rise from Luke.

"Let's go get those rag-arms!" He leaped over the porch rail and raced toward the makeshift field, war-whooping all the way.

Dave barreled out the back door, soap suds dripping from his hands, and ran across the yard. By the time Bonnie, Darlene and Sueanne arrived with the toddlers in tow, Luke's team was warming up on the field and Tom was writing his team's batting order in the scorebook.

Darlene grabbed a leather mitt from the equipment sack and trotted toward left field after detouring past second base for a kiss from Dave. Catcalls and friendly insults flew through the air as everyone geared up for the game. With a groan, Sueanne sat down on the blanket her husband had spread on the ground, then pulled her children onto what remained of her lap.

Caught up in the excitement, adrenalin pumping

through her, Bonnie double-knotted her sneaker laces and did a couple of deep-knee bends to loosen her muscles. In years past, she'd always batted lead-off, because she was fast enough to steal second base and almost a sure bet to score a run if one of her teammates hit a single.

Aiming a Bronx cheer at Luke, who stood poised for action on the pitcher's mound, she lifted a bat and tested its weight in her hands. Ugh! Heavier than she'd remembered.

His knowing grin when she dropped it annoyed her no end. Picking up a shorter, lighter club she stood off to the side and took some practice swings. Much better. His gaze smoldered with a silent challenge when she assumed her stance and wiggled her rear, exactly as he'd taught her so long ago.

"You're batting last," Tom told her, handing the scorebook to Sueanne before grabbing a club and stepping toward homeplate.

Last! Miffed at his obvious lack of confidence in her ability, she kicked a clump of grass. If only she'd kept her mouth shut earlier . . . the story of my life, she thought glumly, sitting down with her team and awaiting her chance at the plate.

Her turn didn't come in the first inning. Luke struck out the first two batters on six straight pitches and forced the third to hit a weak grounder directly at the first baseman.

"You're playing right field," Tom directed, tossing her a stiff, old mitt to wear before he jogged away.

Right field! Had he forgotten that she used to be the quickest shortstop in three counties? Why, the Widow

Painter could play right field and never draw a deep breath! Choking back her protest, she stomped out to her assigned position and furiously worked the inflexible excuse for a glove onto her hand.

Bonnie finally got to bat in the third inning. Like the majority of her teammates, she struck out, swinging too late at a high-inside hummer. Luke beamed with triumph when she missed, and she glared at him as she marched past the pitcher's mound to resume her fielding position.

It wasn't a game anymore. It was war!

The score was tied at one apiece, thanks to homeruns with nobody on by Luke and Tom when twilight threatened to cut the contest short. Bonnie's team was at bat and she rubbed the rosin bag between her damp palms, nervously aware that she'd be the final out for her side if she didn't get a hit.

The first batter struck out; the second one tattooed a line drive right into Dave's glove. Bonnie stepped up to the plate, her heart pounding wildly beneath her ribs. Luke released a fastball, and she missed it by a country mile.

Her teammates groaned. He grinned. She glowered.

His next pitch, a change-up, had her name written all over it. Bonnie's hands stung clear up to her elbows when she slammed the ball, and Luke's jaw hung slack when he heard the resounding crack. She dropped the bat and raced flat-out toward first base. Safe!

Her teammates shouted. She smiled. He scowled.

Tom picked up his favorite club and faced his best friend, temporarily turned foe. Luke glanced at Bonnie poised on the base path, ready to steal second, and his expression would have soured milk. Tom fouled off the first pitch, and she tagged the base before resuming her running stance.

"Luke's got a real steam on tonight!" a fielder yelled.

Her pulse accelerated when he went into an agile wind-up.

"Smoke him out, Luke!" the shortstop razzed.

She tensed when he threw the ball, sprinted when she heard the smack of the bat, then stopped abruptly when Luke caught the pop-fly for the final out. They called the game because of darkness, ending it in a tie.

Although her muscles protested whenever she moved, Bonnie's elation dulled the pain. She hadn't lost her touch after all these years! It felt wonderful shaking hands with everyone, being part of this big, happy family of good sports.

"Help!" Sueanne cried from her blanket on the ground.

While Tom helped his pregnant wife to her feet, Bonnie and Luke carried the sleeping children to their friends' truck. She refused to dwell on how natural he looked with that little boy in his arms. Nor did she let it feel too right, holding the little girl. Her emotions were tangled enough without wondering what it would have been like if life hadn't thrown them a curve.

"That was a nice hit tonight," Luke complimented as Sueanne and Tom drove away.

"You should have seen your face when I was safe at first." Bonnie laughed.

"I play to win." He shrugged and began climbing the front porch steps. "I always have—I always will."

"Well, right now you're talking to a very sore loser." She moaned, limping alongside him.

"I'll rub yours if you'll rub mine," he offered.

"I hope you're talking about sprained ankles and aching backs," she groaned.

They fell asleep on the living room floor, fully dressed, the unopened bottle of liniment lying on its side between them.

9

Sometime in the night, Bonnie turned to Luke and watched him sleeping. She lay with her arm crooked on the hard floor, pillowing her head while monitoring the even rise and fall of his chest and the slight flare of his nostrils as he breathed.

With her fingertips, she touched the cool skin of his face and felt the beginnings of tomorrow's beard. She wanted him—not for a week, but forever. He stirred, murmuring unintelligibly, then extended a muscular arm and drew her closer. She wanted his children—not until tonight when she'd seen him holding another woman's baby had she realized how desperately she still needed to give him one of their own.

But she mistrusted her body. Miscarriage had been the most personal kind of failure, a physical and emotional trauma that had left her riddled with self-doubt. Except for childhood sniffles and bouts of nausea early in her pregnancy, she'd rarely suffered a sick day in her life. When the doctor had told her she was losing her baby, she'd had no idea how painful it would be or that anger and disappointment would plague her long after leaving the hospital.

Luke rolled from his back onto his side, and Bonnie turned in the same direction. He molded her curves to his vibrant male contours, one large hand possessively cupping her breast while the other pressed flat and warm across her abdomen. He held her as though he would never let her go.

She remembered vividly how bewildered he had looked when the orderly had wheeled her past him, toward the swinging doors that led to the operating room. He had leaned over the surgical cart to tell her something —that he loved her, perhaps?—and the quarry dust clinging to his work shirt had drifted onto her tear-stained face before a nurse pulled him away. She had tried to reach out to him, but they'd taped her arm to an intravenous board and strapped it to the gurney.

Her physical anguish had ended abruptly enough under general anesthesia. When she had awakened alone and unpregnant in recovery, though, her emotional turmoil had just begun.

Because the medical ward was full, they had moved her into a room near the newborn nursery. The well-intentioned remarks of others—"You'll have plenty of healthy children later," or "It was for the best; something was obviously wrong with the baby"—had done more harm than good. No one, it seemed, understood that she grieved for the baby who existed in her mind, although it had been unable to exist independently of her body.

The doctor had sent her home with instructions to rest, abstain from sexual relations and visit his office in six weeks for a check-up. She had left the hospital feeling like a failure, and the events leading up to the divorce had destroyed her already battered ego.

Luke whispered an endearment in his sleep, and Bonnie nestled closer to his hard frame. The midnight train rumbled through town, rocking them gently in its wake. Remarriage, especially when they would be commuting cross-country because of their professional commitments, was a risk in and of itself.

The idea of living alone through the week certainly didn't scare her—she had survived for seven years in a city of strangers and learned some important lessons in self-sufficiency as a result. Nor did the thought of refusing those weekend catering assignments really bother her. The takeout business that her shop did at lunchtime and during the holiday season was incredibly profitable.

What she disliked most about Luke's proposition—she didn't yet consider it a bona fide proposal—was the fact that they would be apart more than they would be together. If they were going to start over, she wanted the stability of sharing the good and the bad on a daily basis. She wasn't the least bit interested in becoming a weekend wife. Dating her husband on Saturday night, then kissing him good-bye on Sunday . . .

Bonnie's eyelids grew heavy. She wanted to make love to him when she felt romantic, fight with him when she was angry, laugh with him when . . . her lashes smudged her cheeks as she fell asleep in Luke's arms.

"Good morning, glory," he greeted softly.

"Already?" she mumbled in disbelief. Bonnie opened one eye to the blinding sunlight, then shut it and sighed. "Already."

"How about it?" Luke pulled her closer, if that was possible, and she received a very rude awakening. "Will you marry me?"

"Sorry," she gasped, "I just got engaged to the liniment bottle."

He reached between them, grabbed the offending bottle and flung it onto the sofa behind him. "How did it get down there?"

"I don't know," she grumbled, rubbing her wounded hip, "but I certainly hope it doesn't kiss and tell."

Luke laughed as he flipped her onto her back and pinned her to the floor with his weight. For a breathless instant he simply stared at her, his expression fiercely possessive, then he slipped his hands beneath her shirt and slowly inched them upward. Bonnie wound her arms around his neck and drew his head down, dizzy with anticipation. Their mouths met at the same moment his fingertips circled her nipples, and the exquisite sensation roused her whole body.

"Sure beats an alarm clock," he murmured.

"Doesn't it, though?" she purred.

"Let's take a shower," he suggested. When her breasts ripened under the caress of his callused palms, he grinned. "On second thought, let's stay right here." His hands slid lower, and her hips arched reflexively as he reached the waistband of her shorts.

Someone, Dave from the sound of it, clomped down the stairs. Luke rolled off her with a frustrated growl and pushed himself into a sitting position. Bonnie scurried to her feet and prayed that the wild-rose bloom in her face would fade before it betrayed her.

"Little brother," Luke hailed through clenched jaws, "you are blessed with an incredibly poor sense of timing."

"So is Darlene," Dave groused as he flopped into the overstuffed recliner he'd apparently claimed for his own. "She's testy as a sore tooth this morning." He plowed a hand through his disheveled hair and frowned.

"What's the matter?" Bonnie asked worriedly.

"Last night after you two went to sleep, I sat in the yard with some of the guys and had a couple of beers, unwinding and cracking jokes. When I came inside, Darlene accused me of being drunk—which I wasn't— then marched upstairs in a huff, threatening to call the whole thing off." He shook his head, as if he still couldn't believe that he'd heard correctly.

"Maybe she was just tired," Luke advised. "After all, you've both been working awfully hard this week."

"Well, that's what I figured, so I went to bed in a forgiving frame of mind," Dave continued. "This morning, though, we came out of our bedrooms at the same time, and she just glared at me like I was the devil incarnate." He scratched his chin, his expression perplexed. "I smiled and told her, in a teasing sort of way, that I sincerely hoped she wasn't planning on packing that flannel nightgown for our honeymoon.

You'd have thought I slapped her or something! She burst out crying and slammed the bedroom door in my face."

"Bridal nerves," Bonnie diagnosed astutely.

"I don't care what you call it, the woman is mean," Dave muttered.

"She's nervous," Bonnie corrected. "I've seen some version of this in almost every wedding I've worked. Once, a prospective couple and I were sitting in the bar where they had met, discussing the reception menu. When he mentioned that he liked almonds, she poured a whole bottle of almond-flavored liqueur on his head, set a match to it and submitted his hair to a flambé."

Luke grimaced comically and Dave crossed his arms over his head in a frantically protective gesture.

"I doused him with my club soda and decided that was probably the end of that," she added. "But believe it or not, they got married two weeks later, right on schedule. The groom wore a toupee and the bride promised to love, honor and quit playing with matches."

"Do me a favor and *don't* tell Darlene that story," Dave pleaded. "I'm not about to wear a wig on my wedding day."

"I'll have a talk with her," Bonnie offered. "In the meantime, you run errands and make yourself scarce today. Give her some breathing room before she takes the big step."

"We'll head into Atlanta, get our shoes shined and have lunch at the Engineers' Club," Luke said. "On the way back, we'll stop and pick up the flower arrangements."

"No beers," Bonnie cautioned. "And be home in time

to shell the walnuts for the fudge frosting." She turned in the direction of the kitchen. "Now, who wants coffee?"

Luke and Dave showered, drank their coffee and left in the Corvette. After bathing and changing her clothes, Bonnie ironed the hand-embroidered tablecloth and counted out plates and silverware in preparation for the reception. Darlene was still sulking upstairs when the real estate agent who was handling the sale of their childhood home rang the doorbell.

"Darlene said I could show the house this morning if we'd be quick about it," the middle-aged realtor explained.

While he gave the young couple with him the grand tour, Bonnie mixed up the dough for her potato rolls and set it to rise. Although the guest list was small, only fifteen people including the minister, she considered this reception more important than any society function or professional event she'd ever catered. It was more than a matter of family pride that everything be perfect tomorrow. Remembering her own unplanned-for wedding day, she was determined that Darlene would treasure hers as one of the happiest days of her life.

The real estate agent escorted his clients out the front door after promising that they'd be in touch later with a counteroffer to the asking price of the house. Bonnie poured the marinade off the briskets and smothered the meat with sliced Bermuda onions as Darlene had requested. That done, she covered the baking dishes with foil and placed them in a low-temperature oven.

She had just started upstairs with the intention of having her heart-to-heart talk with her sister when the doorbell rang again.

"Mrs. Painter," Bonnie greeted, feeling guilty because she'd forgotten the widow was coming to call, "how nice to see you."

"Can't stay long." Her wrinkled face wreathed in smiles, the spry little woman picked up a woven willow basket she'd set on the porch and stepped inside. "I just couldn't let the week go by, though, without paying my respects."

Bonnie knew the visit would last at least an hour, but remembered well that the widow had always found time for her. "Will you have a cup of coffee?"

"Don't mind if I do." Mrs. Painter led the way into the kitchen.

"What's in the basket?" Bonnie asked after they were seated at the table with the mugs of steaming coffee that she'd poured each of them.

"The final payment on my new roof." Lifting the lid, she took out a sealed Mason jar. "Luke wouldn't take my money when he finished the job last fall, but he said he would let me keep him in canned goods for a while. This month he gets leather breeches beans, chow chow and some pear honey for his sweet tooth."

"It sounds to me like he's getting the best end of that deal." Bonnie was well acquainted with Mrs. Painter's canning talent. Hardly a week of her youth had passed that the widow hadn't rounded out the family meals with a special treat from her unusual garden—unusual because it was planted by the signs of the zodiac.

"It was a fair enough swap," Mrs. Painter replied. "As in any successful relationship, we each gave a little of ourselves in the bargain."

Bonnie just smiled and sipped her coffee. She had

wondered how long it would take this dear, unabashed meddler to tip her hand.

Mrs. Painter set the jar back in the basket, then peered through her trifocals at Bonnie's ringless hands, which wrapped around her coffee mug. Although too polite to pry outright, her bright blue gaze glittered hopefully. "You know, I bottled some red grape wine seven years ago this summer, and it's just been aging in the rack ever since."

A silence fell between them again, and Bonnie nibbled her lower lip. Whenever one of her "kids" married, Mrs. Painter put up a bottle of wine which she then presented to the couple on the occasion of their first child's birth. To Bonnie's knowledge, she and Luke were the only twosome who'd never collected. She stood and deliberately changed the subject. "I'd better punch down the dough for my rolls."

Mrs. Painter didn't pursue the matter. She sipped her coffee and shared her version of the local news, spicing it up with her unique brand of humor.

"Darlene tells me you have artificial knees now," Bonnie mentioned when she managed to get a word in edgewise.

"I sure do." The widow raised her skirt, proudly exposing her scars, and chuckled. "I won't be doing any fan dances, but thanks to medical science getting ahead of God on my behalf, I'm still able to tend my garden and help my kids when they need me."

"Sueanne told me that you'd be staying with her children when the twins are born." Bonnie covered the dough and put the bowl in the refrigerator where it would remain until morning, when she would shape it into rolls and then let them rise again before baking. "She also said that her mother and Tom's mother both offered to come, but Jon and Vicki wouldn't hear of anybody but you taking care of them."

"I'm just grateful the good Lord saw fit to let me enjoy another generation." Mrs. Painter shuffled to her feet, preparing to leave. "It's been nice visiting with you, darling. Give Luke my regards when you give him the basket."

"Will do," Bonnie promised, walking her to the door.

On the porch, Mrs. Painter finally returned to the real purpose of her visit. "Young wine and first love, if sampled too soon, can leave a bitter aftertaste."

"How well I know," Bonnie agreed ruefully.

The elderly woman descended the steps at a careful pace before having the last word, as had always been her way. "I saved your bottle, Bonnie, believing that the wait would enhance the flavor."

Bonnie was so touched that she couldn't form a reply.

"Tell Darlene and Dave that their wine went into the rack this morning." Mrs. Painter walked toward the road, the spring in her step belying both her eighty years and the surgery that she'd recently endured. When she reached the heat-hazed asphalt, the spritely dowager turned and called, "It's a rosé—light and bubbly, just like them."

Bonnie nodded and waved, wondering for the first time exactly what recipe Mrs. Painter had bottled when she and Luke had eloped seven years ago. A deep, brooding burgundy? A ripe red port? She chuckled. The widow had acquired a rather notorious reputation in these parts for adjusting the sugar content of her homemade wines. Whatever she'd put away, it probably had enough kick by now to knock the shoes off a draft horse.

No sooner had Bonnie shut the door than the telephone rang. It was the minister, confirming that he would stop by the house around seven-thirty that evening for a quick rehearsal of tomorrow's ceremony. She agreed in a slightly harried voice, then once again started upstairs.

Darlene was gone. After searching the second story, Bonnie realized that her sister had most likely slipped away unnoticed during Mrs. Painter's visit. Filled with foreboding, she re-entered Darlene's bedroom.

On the floor in front of the wardrobe sat an open suitcase, empty except for the neatly folded flannel nightgown that Dave had mentioned this morning. She smiled as she imagined Darlene defiantly packing the soft cotton garment, torn between releasing the familiar past and embracing the uncertain future.

Caught in the throes of a similar conflict, Bonnie understood perfectly. She left everything untouched. Returning a few minutes later she placed her wedding present to Darlene, an apricot silk nightgown, in the suitcase. The new laid beside the old, and the choice belonged to Darlene.

Luke and Dave were laughing and joking when they came home several hours later. After she put the wedding corsages they brought into the basement refrigerator, Bonnie poured three glasses of iced tea and told them as calmly as possible about Darlene's disappearance.

"I'm certain there's no cause yet for alarm," she concluded, sounding much more confident than she felt.

"She's probably wandered off somewhere to think and has simply lost track of the time."

Dave sat crestfallen, confusion clouding his hazel eyes. "If she's developed cold feet, why doesn't she just say so instead of—"

"Let's assume at this point that she's only suffering a slight chill," Luke injected sensibly. He took Bonnie's hand, and her fears receded as she absorbed his strength. "Now, do you know of any place she might have gone?" he asked Dave. "A special spot, maybe, where the two of you have been before?"

Thinking of their own loving circle, Bonnie felt her pulse accelerate. As if he'd read her mind, Luke increased the pressure of his grip. They waited quietly, hands joined, for his brother to begin supplying clues to her sister's possible whereabouts.

"West of the waterfall, there's a little cove where we usually have picnic suppers and such," he murmured. Dave flashed a brilliant smile then and slapped his palm on the tabletop. "I'm sure she's there—that's where I proposed to her. Why don't I walk over and see for myself?"

"Frankly, I think this is a woman-to-woman situation." Luke glanced at Bonnie, seeking confirmation.

She nodded and stood. "I said I'd talk to her, and I will."

At the back door, Dave caught her arm and stopped her. "Tell Darlene that regardless of what she's decided . . ." His voice cracked, and he cleared his throat. "I love her."

Luke walked over and clapped his younger brother on

the shoulder. "Dave and I will be elbow deep in walnut shells by the time you two are finished talking."

Bonnie left as they were rolling up their sleeves and hiked westward across the meadow. The waterfall sprayed her with a lightly refreshing mist but she didn't pause to enjoy it. When she found Darlene in the hickory-shaded cove, her knees nearly buckled with relief. Sitting down beside her in the thick grass, she scolded softly, "I don't know whether to hug you or slug you."

"One of each would probably do us both a world of good right about now," Darlene replied in a stuffy-nosed tone. While her fingers plucked nervously at the blades of grass, she closed her puffy-lidded eyes. "Did Dave tell you that this is where he proposed to me?"

"Yes," Bonnie admitted, gently caressing the back of her sister's fine-boned hand.

Darlene tensed and gave a small, uncomfortable laugh. "What else did he tell you?"

"That he loves you," she answered truthfully.

Her sister promptly burst into tears. "I—I'm sorry," she stammered between sobs, "I know that I've been terribly unfair to all of you, behaving like a spoiled brat, but . . ." She broke off, her face bathed in tears.

Bonnie wrapped her arms tenderly around Darlene and let her cry. Moisture beaded on her own lashes but she blinked it away, determined to remain strong in her sister's hour of need.

"I'm frightened," Darlene whispered hoarsely. "What if it doesn't work out and we wind up divorced in a few years?"

"You can't predict that sort of thing," Bonnie replied honestly. "All you can do is try your best to prevent it."

Darlene sighed forlornly. "I wish there were a magic formula written down somewhere that I could read along with all those marriage manuals that the minister gave us."

"Doesn't everybody?" Bonnie released her sister and smoothed the tangled brown hair off her troubled brow. "From my own experience, I know that a wedding license isn't issued with a gilt-edged guarantee. Mine was just a piece of paper, easily shredded in anger. Yours might prove equally flimsy. Then again, it might wear like pig iron. As trite as it sounds, only time will tell."

"I always believed that mama and daddy had a happy marriage." Darlene pulled her knees up under her chin, showing a girlish vulnerability. "I wonder what they did right?"

"If I had to guess, I'd say they communicated—both talking and listening. And they were friends as well as lovers." Bonnie smiled poignantly. "They never knew it, but one night I sat out on the porch swing watching them play Scrabble on the living room floor. Mama spelled out a word—a dirty one, judging from the look on daddy's face, and—"

"*Mama* did that?" Darlene squeaked. When Bonnie nodded, her eyes sparkled curiously. "What happened next?"

"Daddy jumped to his feet." Bonnie snapped her fingers. "Then he literally raced mama upstairs to the bedroom. I felt the vibration of the door slamming shut from the porch."

"Well, what did she spell?" Darlene demanded with a giggle.

"Beats me." Bonnie shrugged. "I crept in later, but they had kicked the board and scattered most of the tiles as they left the room. The only letters left that even remotely resembled a word spelled 'snork.'"

They looked at each other and burst into laughter, collapsing backwards into heaps of uncontrolled hilarity.

"Snork!" Darlene hooted, holding her sides as if they hurt.

"I spent a solid week with my nose buried in every dictionary I could find." Bonnie punctuated the confession with a hiccup.

"And did it really have a definition?" Darlene gasped.

"It's a snoring sound." Bonnie chuckled. "For years, whenever I heard a woman complaining because her husband snored, I immediately pictured our straightlaced mother hiking up her skirts and tearing up those stairs, hell-bent for the bedroom."

When their mirth eventually subsided, they lay still in the grass for a long, peaceful moment. A breeze so soft it might have been a lover's sigh rustled the leaves overhead, while the waterfall babbled merrily as an innocent child.

"I'm a virgin," Darlene admitted bluntly. "Isn't that crazy?"

"Crazy?" Bonnie repeated. She sat up, frankly astonished, and shook her head. "No, it's wonderful. It's—it's incredible."

"Not according to my girl friends," Darlene responded tartly.

"Are you sorry that you waited?" Bonnie ventured.

"No." Darlene grinned mischievously. "The only thing I'm sorry about is that I told my girl friends."

"I feel rather silly asking you this," Bonnie began uncertainly, "but do you have any—well, any questions?"

Darlene sat up and gave the matter careful consideration. "Yes, I do have a question." She scrambled to her feet and brushed off the faded seat of her jeans. "What's for dinner?"

Relieved beyond words, Bonnie stood and aimed a fond smile in her sister's direction. "Now that you've mentioned it, I'm starved."

They left the heavily shaded cove and a vermillion dusk flooded the newly shorn meadow. Halfway home they broke into a run, racing each other and shouting "Snork!" at the top of their lungs.

"What did you do with the extra fudge?" Luke asked later between lazy kisses on her bare, moonlit breasts.

"I poured it into a plate, cut it into squares and gave it to the kids for a midnight snack." Bonnie twined her fingers in his sable-thick hair as his mouth left deliciously sweet kisses around each rosy crest. "I still can't believe that I stirred up a batch-and-a-half."

He laughed. "Did you see the look on Darlene's face when she peeked into the pan? Too much!"

She kneaded his shoulder muscles as he slid lower between her shapely ivory thighs. "She said 'What a waste of sugar,' and started licking the spoon."

"Mmm . . ." He cupped her slender hips in his hands and stole her breath away with his plundering tongue.

Bonnie spiraled wildly with every warm, seductive

stroke. She peaked with a sob, and still she yearned for the physical union that would sweep them both away. Luke moved lithely, taking possession as their bodies melded and their spirits fused.

He rocked her slowly, prolonging the tempest that raged inside her. She watched his eyes glaze with pleasure when her hips arched against him, heard her name expelled hoarsely from his lips as breath mingled with breath. His mouth claimed hers, his tongue matching the passionate rhythm of their bodies. Her arms and legs held him tightly, receiving the whole of him and giving all of herself in return.

Time lost its meaning as their storm reached its breaking point. And when at last they were spent, mindless with the wonder of fulfillment, it seemed that the world had surely come to the same shattering end.

The stars winked through the window when Bonnie eased out of bed. She tiptoed across the room, casting a moonshadow over Luke's soundly sleeping frame, then belted her lacy wrapper around her slim waist. Glancing back over her shoulder, she opened the door and slipped into the hall. Her bare feet instinctively avoided the floorboards that creaked and the steps that squeaked as she padded stealthily downstairs.

How could she leave him? She picked up her purse and carried it into the kitchen. Removing her leather appointment book, Bonnie studied it carefully in the moonlight spilling across the formica table. A total of four free days in the next two months, she noted with a dismal sigh. It wasn't going to work out the way he'd planned it.

She didn't want to spend her life making up for any more time than they'd already lost.

Her return ticket envelope stuck out of the side pocket, where she'd placed it for safekeeping during her stay. When she reached absently to tuck it deeper, her fingers found the handkerchief that Luke had loaned her the other day. Something borrowed. Someone blue. The idle pun brought a poignant smile to her lips, and she impulsively folded the mascara-stained linen back into her purse. He wouldn't miss it.

Just how many other times had Luke been there when she'd needed a helping hand? She closed her eyes, recalling a thousand different ways he'd taught her the meaning of trust.

And what had he ever asked of her in return? Bonnie's eyes flew open wide with disbelief, and she felt the monstrous hand of guilt crushing the breath from her body. When Luke had needed her most, she'd failed him. Wrapped her heart in a selfish shroud of sorrow and refused to share his pain. Rather than help him, she'd hurt him worse.

She stood abruptly and the kitchen clock cuckooed three times when she pushed purposefully through the swinging doors. How was it that Mrs. Painter had defined a successful relationship? Each of the partners giving something of themselves in the bargain? Close enough. The stairs had never seemed steeper nor the halls darker. Yet Bonnie's footsteps quickened with confidence as she neared the bedroom. She gripped the glass doorknob and smiled, coming to terms with her love for Luke.

10

·°°°°°°°°°°°·

Darlene's wedding day dawned with a beautiful, maidenly blush.

Although Bonnie hadn't slept a wink after returning to bed, she was the first one up. Wearing a general's air of authority and a navy terry-cloth jumpsuit that hugged her figure, she began rousing the others. She also came dangerously close to inciting total rebellion.

"Five more minutes in that bathroom, Dave, and you can register it as your new voting address."

"If you've really outgrown your wedding gown, Darlene, fifty sit-ups this morning won't do your waistline a damn bit of good."

"Don't push your luck, Luke. Another pinch like that last one and—ouch! I'm warning you, Luke . . ."

When her sleep-tousled and slightly hostile crew finally gathered in the hallway she herded them downstairs, issuing orders every step of the way. "Coffee and toast for breakfast, then it's everybody into the act." She synchronized her watch with the kitchen clock. "Our guests should start arriving in four hours flat."

"Four hours!" Darlene gasped, her eyes widening with alarm. She stirred an extra spoonful of sugar into her coffee cup. "How on earth will we get it all done, plus make ourselves presentable in *four* hours?"

"I'll bet our favorite drill sergeant already has the schedule figured out down to the second," Luke teased. He stretched, leisurely defying the brisk pace she was attempting to set. "In fact, I'd stake my skyscraper on it."

Bonnie's heart somersaulted and her glance skipped nervously around the sunlit kitchen, avoiding contact with his good-natured gaze. If he thought she sounded organized right now, just wait until he heard the details of that *other* timetable she'd devised!

"Can somebody press this shirt collar so it lies flat?" Dave set the iron aside and heaved a frustrated sigh.

"I just showed you how to do that last month," Darlene reminded him, crunching off a corner of her generously buttered toast.

"I forgot," he admitted with a sheepish grin, holding up the scorched and mangled material. "Maybe I'd better start over. I'll run downstairs and throw it into the washing machine."

"Low suds," Darlene instructed between bites, "and a little bleach."

"Far be it from me to interrupt domestic democracy in the making," Luke said, "but why don't you just borrow one of my shirts?"

Judging from the expression on Dave's face, it was the best idea that he'd heard in a month of Sundays.

"They're in the hall closet," Luke directed. "Take your pick."

"We'll drop it by the laundry when he's done with it," Darlene promised as she stood and followed her soon-to-be husband through the swinging doors.

Bonnie dusted her hands with flour and began shaping her yeast-rich dough into rolls. "I think I'll buy Dave a dozen permanent press shirts and tell Darlene that they're *her* wedding present, too."

Luke stood behind her and fit his lean male length against her softly rounded bottom and sleek legs. His arms easily circled her slender waist, and he interfered with her breathing ability when he nuzzled the sensitive spot behind her earlobe. "All *I* want for a wedding present is—"

"We've got a problem, folks," Darlene announced dramatically.

Dave trailed along behind her, the sleeves of Luke's shirt dangling a good two inches below his hands. "I tried it on for size and—"

"What's burning?" Bonnie demanded, an acrid smell suddenly searing her nostrils.

"My shirt!" Dave yelped. He dashed across the kitchen and snatched the smoking wad off the board, where he'd dropped it too close to the hot iron. "My best shirt," he groaned. "It's ruined."

"No wedding is complete without at least one catastrophe," Bonnie consoled. She pointed a doughy finger at Darlene. "Run upstairs and find a needle and a spool of white thread. When it's time to dress, we'll tack up the sleeves of the borrowed shirt, and nobody will ever know the difference."

She arched an eyebrow at Dave, who was still mourning his charred shirt. "Go hang the one you're wearing in the closet before something happens to *it*, and toss the one you're holding into the rag bag."

They both scampered off to do exactly as she'd directed, no questions asked. Bonnie turned, flush with success, and started to give Luke an assignment.

"A cool head and a warm body," he murmured, drawing her into his arms again. "What a combination."

She tipped her head back and met his admiring gaze. "It's called the art of survival, actually. Any caterer worth her salt learns quickly that—" Bonnie felt her zipper sliding open and looked down in surprise at the front of her jumpsuit. "What in the name of blue blazes are you doing?"

"Well, you got out of bed and into your clothes so fast this morning, I didn't have a chance to . . ." His words were muffled softly then in the lush spill of her breasts as he freed them from the terry cloth.

It was totally insane, standing there unzipped in broad daylight, but she reveled in every crazy second. Bonnie curled her toes as wildfire swooped through her veins, and arched closer still to his hard body as spears of pleasure pierced her nerve endings. Needing him nearer yet, she cradled his head between her hands and . . . her hands!

She quickly pulled them away, laughing at the sticky palm prints she'd left. "Don't look now but you just went cauliflower ears one better."

He raised his head, his smile as warm as his tongue

had been against her skin. "Let's set a date," he suggested in a husky voice. "We'll announce it this afternoon while our families and friends are here."

Bonnie's thoughts scattered like dandelion seeds in a sudden puff of wind. This was neither the time nor the place to spring her surprise on him. She'd wanted to wait until they were alone tonight, knowing it would take a while to convince him that her idea made more sense than his. . . .

Regret shadowed Luke's chiseled features as the silence spun out. "You've changed your mind."

"Darn it, I didn't even *make up* my mind until three o'clock this morning!" She stamped her foot, frustrated by the unexpected turn of events.

"What?" He drew back as if she'd slapped him.

Bonnie spun away and rezipped the front of her jumpsuit, piqued that they'd taken such a foolish, adolescent risk. "I love you, Luke, and I do want to marry you. But I don't want to be a part-time wife."

"Because you don't trust me," he concluded dully.

"Because I don't trust *myself*," she corrected in a soft voice.

"What the hell is that supposed to mean?" His tone echoed his confusion. "I thought we'd already settled—"

Bonnie shook her head, silencing him. She gripped the edge of the flour-coated countertop, groping for the words that would best clarify her concerns. Her thoughts didn't gel, however, until her hands were washed and busy again creating cloverleaf rolls from the shapeless lump of dough.

"For reasons I can't even explain, I never doubted myself professionally." Her lips curved in a self-mocking smile. "It may sound brash, but it's true. When I climbed off that bus in New York City seven years ago, I just knew that with a lot of hard work and a little bit of luck, I'd eventually have half of New York eating out of my hand."

"We fixed the sleeves of Luke's shirt," Darlene interrupted, pushing through the swinging doors. "I pinned them and Dave sewed them."

"Good for you," Bonnie said. "Now you can rearrange the living room furniture so that there's an aisle from the bottom of the stairs to the front of the fireplace."

"But if we rearrange the furniture, we'll have to run the sweeper again," Darlene objected. When she saw the adamant expression on Bonnie's face, she turned on her heel and marched out of the kitchen in an indignant huff.

"Maybe I'm being too hard on her," Bonnie worried aloud as she spread clean towels over her roll pans and left the dough to rise. "After all, it *is* her wedding day."

"You warned her that a ceremony at home meant a lot of last-minute preparations and everybody pitching in." Luke rolled up his shirt sleeves, ran water in the sink and began washing the breakfast dishes. "I just hope that Dave hasn't forgotten how to run the vacuum cleaner."

Bonnie laughed, then reached into the cupboard and removed both a maple cutting board and a china meat platter. Ducking into the pantry, she grabbed the square teakwood case that she'd carried on the plane from New York. Luke whistled appreciatively when he saw the carving knives, custom made with blades of high carbon steel and handles of carved ivory.

"These are my good-luck charms," she explained, returning to their earlier topic of conversation. "I ordered them the same day that I signed the lease agreement for my shop." She shook her head, amazed now by her audacity then. "By the time I'd paid for city licenses, three months' rent and fees for plumbers and electricians, I could barely afford to stock the shelves."

"You must have done something right," Luke commented as he scraped and scrubbed the countertop where she'd shaped her rolls. "To hear Darlene tell it, you were practically an overnight success."

"I did all the work, but Lady Luck deserves a lot of the credit." Bonnie took the briskets from the refrigerator where she'd put them to cool after cooking. "Despite the fact that every day was a sellout, I knew so little about costs and even less about pricing that I was operating at a loss." She picked up a carving knife and poised it over a slab of beef. "One of my regular customers was a reporter for *New York* magazine. She told me I should raise my prices, which I did. And then she wrote an article, actually more of a filler, commending my 'silver spoons'—"

"Isn't that the name of your catering service?" he asked.

She nodded and began slicing the brisket cross-grain. "I adopted it in her honor, and it caught on almost immediately. After the article ran, my phone started ringing and never stopped." Bonnie grinned. "The first month that I turned a profit, I hired a bookkeeper—a frugal soul who squeezes a nickel so tight, the buffalo bellows as loud as my suppliers when she negotiates with them."

"The living room is ready!" Darlene shouted to be heard over the roar of the carpet sweeper that Dave was running. "I arranged the furniture so everyone can watch us coming down the stairs and still see us exchanging our vows in front of the fireplace. I even fixed up a corner where Uncle Ike can stand while he plays his fiddle."

"I certainly hope your Uncle Ike remembers that this is a wedding and not a square dance," Bonnie teased Luke, brandishing her knife for emphasis. "The last time I heard him play, every other song sounded just like 'Turkey in the Straw.'"

"If he forgets where he is, we'll just do-si-do down the stairs and allamande left at the aisle." Darlene grabbed a piece of beef and danced a silly jig, her face flushed with excitement.

"We'll put out the flowers last thing so they'll be fresh when the guests arrive." Bonnie slapped Darlene's hand when she reached for another slice of the tender meat. "You go on upstairs and take your shower. As soon as we're through in here, I'll come up and help you get dressed."

Dave and Darlene met each other coming and going through the swinging doors. After a quick kiss and a few affectionate words, they parted company until the ceremony. Watching them, Bonnie was struck by their innocence, their confidence, and she silently wished them smoother sailing than she and Luke had experienced.

"Can I use the Corvette to go get a couple of sacks of ice?" Dave's freckled face wore the same high color that Darlene's had. He caught the keys his brother tossed, then hurried out of the house to run his errand.

When they were alone again, Luke took the carving knife and expertly sliced the second slab of beef. Bonnie arranged the meat on the platter, garnishing it with parsley sprigs and cherry tomatoes. While she worked, she summoned her courage. Where did a woman begin baring her soul to the man she loved?

"Some of my insecurity now stems from the fact that I was so young and uninformed when I miscarried, so confused when we divorced." She bit her lower lip and met his steady brown gaze, imploring his understanding. "I was a girl with a woman's problems. And having been weaned on fairy tales where everyone lives happily ever after, I was also terribly ignorant of realistic solutions."

Finished arranging the platter, she sealed it with clear plastic wrap and set it in the refrigerator with the salads and fresh vegetables that she'd already prepared. Luke washed the knife and the cutting board, then wiped the counter clean. Except for the rolls, which would be baked immediately before serving, the reception was ready ahead of schedule.

"What I'm trying to say is that my business was the child I'd failed to deliver." Bonnie accepted the cup of coffee that Luke had poured for her and sat down at the table. "No new mother ever took more pride in her baby's first tooth or first step than I took in the growth of my catering service. As ridiculous as it sounds, I even slept on a cot in the back of the shop for a while so I'd be available in case of an emergency."

"You never were one to do things halfway." Luke stood behind her chair, slowly massaging her stiffly held shoulders.

"Well, Mr. Win-Or-Die-Trying," she teased, "aren't you a fine one to talk?"

"With our attitudes, it's no wonder we wound up

divorced." His voice was husky with emotion. "We were more like Kamikaze pilots than husband and wife."

"It's a miracle we lived to talk about it." Bonnie sighed, recalling the marital battles which could have ended in compromise or with an apology if they each hadn't been so bent on being right.

"Remember the year that your peach cobbler won second place in the 4-H cooking contest?" His strong, sure hands slid to her nape.

Bonnie nodded, relaxing as he deftly dissolved the tension in her muscles. "I was so mad, I wanted to spit."

"And I was so fed up with peach cobbler by the time the next contest rolled around, I was tempted to bribe the judges." His long, gifted fingers found and relieved a knot at the base of her neck.

"I won the blue ribbon," she reminded him proudly.

"But I got the best prize of all." He bent over, his warm breath fanning her face. "And it was sweeter than anything those judges had ever sampled."

"Help!" Dave stood on the back porch holding a bag of ice in each arm.

Luke opened the door, grabbed a dripping plastic sack and stored it in the kitchen freezer compartment. While Dave carried the second bag to the basement, Bonnie mopped up the puddles on the floor with paper towels.

"I saw Tom at the store," Dave mentioned when he came upstairs. "He said that he and Sueanne would be here early to greet and seat the guests while we're all getting ready for the ceremony."

"Did you tell him that we bought extra film yesterday for his camera?" Luke asked.

"I sure did." Dave grabbed a piece of cold toast off the

plate sitting in the center of the table. "I'll go shower and shave now so the bathroom will be free whenever you are."

After the doors banged shut behind his little brother, Luke encircled Bonnie's waist with his hands and she rested hers on his broad shoulders. In the most round-about way possible, they'd finally arrived at the issue that remained unsettled between them. Easing into the truth, she delivered her good news first.

"I'm coming home, Luke," she whispered. "This fall, after I've phased out my catering service in Manhattan."

"Are you sure you can give up your business?" He lifted her chin with his index finger. "Now that I know how much—"

"I'm *not* going out of business," she clarified. "I'm simply relocating." She held his face between her palms, stroking the high planes of his cheekbones with her thumbs. "Until the other day, I hadn't realized that Atlanta was undergoing such a corporate boom."

"It's got a case of the sprawls, all right," he agreed. "Almost every major firm as well as a host of foreign companies has opened a branch here."

"Well, corporations mean office parties, trade conventions, press breakfasts and such," she explained. "Those are my favorite kind of catering assignments. Not only do the clients appreciate the quality, but they generally pay their bills when presented with them."

"You can set up shop in my building, if you like." Bending forward, he caressed her lips with his. "We might even work out an *arrangement* on the rent."

"Actually, I was thinking of buying my own building." Her voice quivered with the delicious havoc his mouth was creating. "One story, perhaps, but with adequate space for a full-service gourmet kitchen and—"

He silenced her with a quick kiss. "You can worry about that later, after we're married. Right now our main concern is setting a date, scheduling blood tests and arranging for a license."

It was time for the bad news. Her heart pounded convulsively against her ribs and she swallowed the lump forming in her throat. "Luke, how does the idea of an October wedding strike you?"

"October?" he repeated, disbelief flaring in his eyes. "Frankly, it strikes me as one hell of a long and unnecessary wait."

"It's only five months or so," she reasoned, "and we'll both be busy, you with that shopping center project that you've bid on and me with—"

"What is it, Bonnie?" he demanded. "Why can't we be married and busy at the same time?" His expression darkened ominously. "Or is this just a polite way of saying 'So long, chump' and skipping town on me again?"

She stiffened, hurt by his obvious mistrust, and freed herself from his embrace. "How can you even believe me capable of such a thing after what we've shared the past few days and nights?"

A faintly mocking smile touched his mouth. "Well, you aren't exactly famous hereabouts for your farewell speeches."

"Why is it that *I'm* supposed to forgive and forget, but *you're* not?" she demanded. "Why do all the concessions have to come from me?" She whirled away from him, distraught. "Do you honestly think it was an easy decision for an eighteen-year-old girl to make, leaving her home and family . . ." Her voice broke then, but her posture was proud as she started toward the swinging doors.

He grabbed her arm and spun her around. "Bonnie, wait—"

"No, Luke." She pulled free of his grip and looked straight into his eyes before she left the kitchen. "I won't fight with you about this—it's too important to me. If you love me, *you wait.*"

Upstairs, Darlene was in a terrible dither. Wearing only her slip and pantyhose, she wandered into Bonnie's bedroom with her arms outstretched like a scarecrow's. "When I put my arms down I sweat," she moaned miserably. "And I can't get dressed until I fix my hair. But I put so much conditioner on after I shampooed that I can't fix my hair."

"Sit," Bonnie commanded firmly after stepping out of the shower. She wrapped her own dripping hair in a thick towel, slipped into her robe and went to work transforming her cute kid sister into an utterly sensational bride.

"It's a miracle," Darlene marveled, staring at her starry-eyed reflection in the full-length mirror later. The very picture of old-fashioned loveliness, she wore a white crepe dress lavishly frosted with lace. Her shiny brown hair was pulled into a charming chignon at the nape of her neck, while a few loose wisps floated around her oval face. "I can't believe it's really me. For the first time in my life, I feel beautiful."

"You *are* beautiful," Bonnie insisted.

"So are you," Darlene replied sincerely.

It was true, Bonnie admitted without vanity. Despite the scene with Luke, or perhaps because of it, her complexion glowed radiantly and her eyes sparkled with an extra brilliance. Her crepe dress, a soft, tiger-lily shade, clung to her shoulders while the kerchief hem flirted fashionably around her knees.

They posed for pictures, some silly and some serious.

"Thank you for the nightgown," Darlene sniffled.

"You're welcome." Bonnie's voice was equally shaky.

"And thank you for being the best friend any woman could have," Darlene added tremulously.

They hugged each other very tightly then and dabbed at the tears only sisters can share.

Her expression puzzled, Sueanne hurried into the bedroom as fast as impending motherhood would allow. "What, pray tell, am I supposed to do with all that food?"

"Leave it in the refrigerator," Bonnie instructed.

"But the refrigerator is full," Sueanne countered.

"Of course it is . . ." Bonnie turned her head, distracted by the noise. With the door open, she could hear that Uncle Ike had rosined up his fiddle bow for what she prayed would prove a wedding song of sorts. She also heard the voices. Male and female, laughing and talking louder than a convention of human buzz saws.

"You know how it is around here," Sueanne explained with a shrug. "Everybody is just one big happy family. Luke and Dave are down there now glad-handing left and right."

Darlene dashed to the window and peeked outside. "Why, I'll bet there's thirty people lined up on the sidewalk!" she squealed. "And they've all brought covered dishes!" She swirled, skirt and hair flying, and clapped her hands. "Do you suppose they've come to give us a charivari?"

Bonnie crossed to the window and drew back the drape. Friends and neighbors she'd known all her life but hadn't seen in years stood patiently in the sun. They'd come to pay their respects, she realized, and say a proper good-bye to the girls who'd grown up playing in the meadow.

She allowed herself a brief moment of shame for having forgotten the ways of her raising, then turned to her excited sister with a smile. "Don't quote me, but I think there's one whale of a charivari taking shape today."

Nervous giggling punctuated their last-minute flurry of preparations. Bonnie repinned her sister's hair, anchoring it more securely this time. Darlene couldn't find her shoes to save her soul. After five minutes of frantic searching, she located them where she'd left them—in a box on the floor of her closet. Sueanne lumbered up and down the stairs so often, Bonnie worried that she might well deliver her twins between progress reports.

Finally, the wedding hour arrived. Uncle Ike's fiddle serenaded sweetly. Wildflower bouquets blossomed fragrantly. The guests sat or stood in quiet anticipation. Bonnie and Darlene descended the stairs, each to meet the man she loved.

11

~oooooooooo~

"For richer or for poorer," the minister intoned solemnly.

Bonnie looked at Luke, standing across the semi-circle that the wedding party had formed in front of the fireplace. He cut a striking figure in a tropical-weight suit, custom-tailored to those incredible shoulders and his impressive stature. A starched and snowy shirt collar broke the tawny blend of face and fabric, accentuating the healthy hue of his skin and the bronzed thickness of his hair.

A wry smile curved her lips. When they'd eloped, he hadn't even *owned* a suit. He'd worn a clean pair of jeans and a neatly pressed plaid shirt, while she'd let out the seams of her high school graduation dress to accommodate the weight she'd gained. . . .

"In sickness and in health," Darlene repeated distinctly.

Did Luke still suffer those awful hayfever attacks when the goldenrod flowered and the ragweed flew? Had he noticed the spidery white scar where she'd carved her hand instead of the Chateaubriand while catering an intimate dinner party one night last fall? Besides climbing scaffolds and playing a mean game of softball, what other kind of exercise kept him in such fine physical shape? Did he know that every evening, rain or shine, she slipped into her sneakers and walked from her shop to her small co-op apartment on the East side of Manhattan?

"With this ring, I thee wed," Dave vowed gravely.

Bonnie's head throbbed with memories. Sunlight glinting off gold whenever she'd hung their laundry to dry on the clothesline. Her girl friends cooing enviously when they would stop by to share the news of which college sorority they'd pledged. The compassionate nurse sliding her ring back onto her finger following the minor surgery which had dealt such a major blow to her ego.

Tears clouded her vision. What had happened to that plain gold band after she'd flung it in Luke's face? She remembered hearing it hit the floor—the hollow *clank* had haunted her dreams off and on for years. Had he even bothered retrieving it, or had it just rolled into a corner and been swept away with her shattered hopes and the morning-after debris?

"I now pronounce you husband and wife." The minister smiled indulgently. "You may kiss, if you'd like."

When Dave and Darlene embraced, there wasn't a dry eye in the room. Had everyone else here felt the same personal impact while listening to the wedding vows? Or were these simply tears of joy for two of their own, now one before God and man?

Bonnie glanced at Luke. Pride softened his chiseled features as he watched the newlyweds. He looked at her and their gazes locked. Her heart hammered expectantly, and her eyes asked but a single question.

Before she could see the answer she sought in those darkly shadowed depths, Uncle Ike stepped between them and the reception got off to a foot-stomping start.

A crowd of well-wishers surged forward, further separating her from Luke. Bonnie shook hands all around, playing the role of hostess to the hilt while gradually working her way toward the kitchen. If anyone noticed the tremor in her voice or the lack of spirit in her smile, they were kind enough not to comment.

Precisely where she lost control of the intimate party that she'd arranged in honor of the bride and groom, Bonnie never really knew. Was it in the dining room, where she discovered Mrs. Painter defying the law of gravity in her stockinged feet atop a stepladder, cheerfully stringing purple and yellow crepe-paper streamers from the chandelier to the ceiling moldings?

"I saved these after the Easter egg roll on the church lawn," the widow explained. "Never dreamed they'd come in so handy this soon."

"I'll bet the doctor who operated on your knees would have a coronary if he could see you right now," Bonnie scolded, hoping the threat struck a little terror where it would do the most good.

Mrs. Painter seemed to give the matter careful consideration before she sniffed haughtily. "What he doesn't know won't hurt him."

Bonnie steadied the ladder while the feisty widow slapped a piece of tape across a streamer. "Please," the younger woman implored, imagining nothing less than total disaster, "let me help."

"Okay," the white-haired wonder agreed, "go organize that crew of casserole queens and leave me alone. I'd like to get done with this before I meet my Maker."

In the kitchen, Bonnie acknowledged that the small reception she'd planned for Dave and Darlene was indeed a thing of the past.

A kettle of large white hominy bubbled on the stove beside a pot of fresh green beans flavored with salt pork. In a huge flat willow basket her potato rolls—baked to a delicate brown—nestled with crispy hush puppies, golden slabs of cornbread and thick slices of buttermilk bread.

Cinnamon-rich peach cobblers, tame gooseberry pies and bowls of carrot pudding shared counter space with the chocolate wedding cake that she'd created. And the platter of brisket she'd prepared ahead of time sat in the center of the formica table surrounded by other serving dishes piled high with fried chicken and sugar-cured ham.

Sueanne had tied a butcher-block apron over her slate-blue maternity smock, kicked off her sensibly heeled sandals and taken charge of the kitchen patrol. She spread her arms wide, blew a russet wisp of hair off her damp forehead and smiled. "Well, what do you think?"

"I think I've been sabotaged," Bonnie teased.

"Roundly and soundly," Sueanne confirmed.

Bonnie plucked a watermelon pickle off a relish tray and plopped the crunchy cube into her mouth. "This room looks like an emergency relief center."

"Like I said earlier, you know how it is around here." Sueanne selected a crisp cucumber spear from the same tray. "Money is scarce, but friends are sacred."

On the verge of tears for the umpteenth time that

week, Bonnie could only nod in agreement. She walked to the sink and stared out the window, thinking of all the brutally lonely holidays she'd spent in strangers' kitchens. Without a husband or family and with no close friends to speak of, she'd always been available for the assignments that other caterers refused because they wanted to be home for the celebration.

She had overworked herself on purpose, funneling every ounce of energy into a business that had eventually become the core of her very existence. What a price she had paid, nurturing profit margins as a substitute for the child she had lost and letting money take the place of love.

Sueanne shooed everyone else out of the kitchen, then stood beside Bonnie at the sink. "You and Luke were always such perfectionists," she mused quietly. "Even as kids, neither of you ever seemed satisfied with second-best."

"Darlene called me the original golden girl the other day, but somehow it didn't seem like much of a compliment," Bonnie admitted in a whisper. "I wonder if she had a nickname for Luke?"

"Well, my daddy generally referred to the two of you as thoroughbreds." Sueanne laughed softly. "I remember one night Tom and I were sitting in my folks' kitchen when you and Luke stopped by after softball practice. The four of us made lemonade from scratch and used up all my mother's sugar—"

"You and I were juniors in high school that spring," Bonnie reminisced. "Luke was captain of his college team, and I was their unofficial cheerleader and scorekeeper."

Sueanne nodded, obviously pleased that Bonnie recalled the occasion. "My daddy joined us for a while and was so impressed, listening while Luke talked about how someday he was going to build bridges all over the world. Then you chimed in and described the tea shop that you intended to open in downtown Atlanta." She chuckled. "Of course, you were also going to marry each other, own the biggest home in the Southeast and raise ten kids in your spare time."

"We didn't miss realizing our professional pipe dreams by much," Bonnie murmured. Her eyes brimming with tears, she tore a paper towel off the roll and used it to blot them. "We fell a little short of our personal goals, though."

"Darn! I brought this up to make a point and instead I've made you cry." Sueanne rapped a fist on the edge of the sink. "I'm sorry."

"Don't be—I want to hear what you have to say." Bonnie managed a watery but convincing smile. "You can't possibly be any harsher than I've been on myself. And the same is probably true of Luke."

"What I've been leading up to is, in all the ways that count both of you were well-prepared for success." Sueanne arched an auburn eyebrow, looking wise beyond her years. "It was failure that caught the two of you off-guard."

"And how," Bonnie agreed wryly.

"If you're going to homestead, girls, build a fence." Mrs. Painter shoved open the swinging doors and stormed into the kitchen. "In case you've forgotten, there's a party of hungry people out there."

The "casserole queens" she'd referred to earlier marched in behind her and began taking the food into the dining room.

"Sueanne." Bonnie stopped her friend in passing. "Did your dad *really* call me a thoroughbred?"

"He sure did," Sueanne affirmed, picking up a plate of molasses cookies to carry out to the table. "He used to say, 'Give Bonnie enough steel wool and she'll knit a stove.' "

"Was that before or after the time I talked you into bleaching your hair and it turned orange?" Bonnie took her pesto salad from the refrigerator and stirred it, then garnished it with tomato wedges.

"I looked like a clown!" Sueanne remembered with a shudder. "Even if my daddy hadn't grounded me, I wouldn't have left the house." She lifted a glass baking dish of macaroni swimming in cream sauce and cheddar cheese. "If my daughter Vicki ever does anything that dumb—"

"*There* you are," Darlene scolded with mock severity as she entered the kitchen. "I should have known, I suppose." With her skirt hoisted up about her knees and her feet bare, she resembled a little girl playing dress-up in her mother's clothes. She grabbed Bonnie's hand and gave it a hearty yank. "Come on, Tom wants to take pictures of the four of us while we're still fairly presentable."

Faces and voices were a blur as her sister practically dragged her into the living room. Tom posed them first in front of the fireplace where they'd held the ceremony. Then he took only the bride and groom, their arms tightly linked and their eyes sparkling with love and laughter.

When Luke moved away from the mantel, he was immediately surrounded by a happy horde eager to have a word with him and share the latest local gossip. Bonnie waited quietly on the fringe of the noisy reunion, feeling like an outsider looking in and wondering whether she could ever truly belong again. Self-consciously, she dropped her gaze to the floor and stepped backwards a few feet. It wouldn't do to act pushy or—

"Now take Bonnie and Luke together," Darlene directed with Dave's full approval.

"Come on, you two." Tom waved them into place.

Bonnie glanced at Luke. His jawline hardened as he noticed that she was standing apart from everyone else. Although her spirits plunged, she raised her chin in challenge. What hurt most was that he hadn't even *tried* to include her.

Luckily, their brief visual deadlock appeared to go unnoticed by the others. Somebody pulled her forward and positioned her beside him while the crowd melted out of the picture.

"Bonnie, you look like you just lost your best friend," Tom chided, peering through the lens.

Maybe I have, she answered silently as she pasted on a false smile for posterity's sake.

"Luke, would it kill you to relax a little?" Tom asked, his patience clearly wearing thin.

Luke shrugged his broad shoulders, loosening up a bit, then eyed her with a frown. "Do you realize that you're the only woman in the house who's still wearing shoes?"

Bonnie breathed a short laugh of disbelief. She didn't

want to argue with him, not now, yet she heard herself issue a challenge. "Does that fact insult your keep-them-barefoot-and-pregnant mentality?"

"One picture," Tom implored.

Luke chuckled, throwing her off-guard, then crouched down so abruptly that she didn't have a chance to consider escape. His strong fingers captured her slender ankle and raised her foot off the floor. She reached down, groping for support but grabbing a handful of his hair by mistake.

He yelped, startling her, and she jerked backward. They both lost their balance and sat down, hard. When it was obvious that pride was the only casualty of their fall, the crowd they'd attracted began applauding.

"Perfect!" Tom took aim and snapped. A blinding flash confirmed that he had frozen their sprawling figures on film.

More applause. Luke grinned wickedly as he reached down and methodically removed her shoes, then tossed them over his shoulder. A boxing-crowd roar—decidedly male, she noted—greeted his action.

Not to be outdone, Bonnie slid her index finger into the knot of his tie and tugged. When the four-in-hand gave, she slipped the silk tie from under his collar and threw it into the air. A soprano ovation rewarded her effort.

They gazed at each other and, of one accord, broke into hearty laughter to the utter delight of the wedding guests.

"Come and get it!" Mrs. Painter yelled from the dining room.

The battle between the sexes ended in a draw. Luke scrambled lithely to his feet, then extended a hand and assisted Bonnie. The hard pressure of his grip shot an exquisite thrill along her arm, and his breath felt warm as summer rain on her face when she stood, two inches shorter than before, in front of him.

For the life of her, she couldn't remember what had started their latest and surely their silliest tiff. She puzzled the matter through from beginning to end and realized that a small miracle had just occurred. They'd smoothed over an area of potential hostility with humor, defusing a conflict before they wounded each other with harmful words and actions. Had they also paved a way for dealing with touchy areas in the future? They couldn't laugh off *everything,* of course, but—

Luke straightened to his full height and looked down just as Bonnie glanced up. She was unaware of what an entrancing portrait she made with her hair floating like honey around her face and her cheeks blooming a wild-berry red. She opened her mouth to tell him how much she loved him, that she would marry him tomorrow if it was so all-fired important to him, and he pressed a silencing finger to her lips.

"Hey, Luke!" Dave shouted. "Get a load of this, will you?"

"Bonnie!" Darlene beckoned. "Quick, come see this."

Duty called and they answered reluctantly. Everyone had crowded around the dining room table, a veritable groaning board of homemade dishes. Mrs. Painter and Sueanne stood near the swinging doors, holding out the friendship quilt that the local sewing bee had pieced and sewn together as a wedding present for Darlene and Dave.

A lump swelled in Bonnie's throat when she closely

inspected the colorful scraps, each embroidered with the name of a woman who'd worked on the keepsake. Fancy-stitched, then bordered and backed with navy blue, the quilt was a visual ballad of sharing that fairly shouted of love.

Looking around the circle of faces, some wrinkled and some smooth, Bonnie knew there were no words that could adequately express her emotions. She also realized that none were necessary. These were her people. They understood. And whether or not Luke found it in his heart to wait for her, she was coming home with a fresh supply of self-esteem in the fall and setting up shop in Atlanta.

"Reverend," Mrs. Painter said as she and Sueanne folded the quilt, "would you say the blessing?"

All afternoon, it seemed there was a conspiracy of sorts on the part of the guests to keep Bonnie and Luke at opposite ends of the house. Luke filled his plate and was immediately hustled out to the front porch where the men whiled away the hours swapping tall tales. The women included her in an equally lengthy kitchen klatch, inquiring politely about New York but obviously content on southern soil.

Darlene and Dave lingered far longer than expected, personally thanking everyone, before announcing that they were leaving on their honeymoon. A round of good-byes followed before they finally made their way outside.

"We're stopping by our house in Atlanta to change clothes and pick up our other luggage," Darlene explained when someone questioned the fact that the two of them had only one suitcase. Pure as her wedding gown of white, she hugged her handmade treasure tightly in her arms. "Besides, we want to put the quilt on our bed before we leave, so it'll be there to greet us when we come home."

"Where's Luke?" Dave's freckled face wore a baffled expression. "We've turned the house and the outbuildings upside down searching for him so we could tell him good-bye."

Bonnie thought she knew, but she wasn't saying any more than was absolutely necessary. She leaned over and whispered in Darlene's ear that she'd go fetch him, then slipped through the house and out the back door. Hiking up her skirt, she raced across the meadow. If she were wrong—no, she couldn't think that way. Not today.

At the bottom of the wooded hill, she paused and drew a calming breath. Twilight lay like a gray velvet mantle over the land while she climbed the slight incline.

Bonnie found Luke leaning against a hickory trunk. The red glow of his cigarette tip guided her through the heavy limbs and bending boughs, into the circle she still considered sacred. Halfway across the clearing, she hesitated and prayed that her voice wouldn't crack when she spoke.

"What are you doing?" she asked softly.

"Practicing my waiting," he answered simply.

Bonnie stood speechless with joy. Those three words told her what she needed to know, and then some. Luke flicked his cigarette to the ground, crushing it with the toe of his leather shoe. Pinecones scuttled underfoot as he met her in the middle.

"I love you." They spoke as one when they embraced, keeping their evergreen commitment at long last. His mouth sought hers and their kiss renewed a trust that was stronger for having been tested.

She tipped her head in curiosity when they drew slightly apart. "Why were you angry with me during the picture-taking session?"

He smiled ruefully, his gaze roaming over her upturned face. "I thought *you* were mad because the formal reception that you'd planned had suddenly turned into a family reunion. And a rather noisy one at that."

"I was *sad*," she confessed in a throbbing whisper. The memory of the moment still hurt. "Everyone was having fun without me. Laughing. Talking. Even gossiping. I felt so excluded. So . . . unnecessary."

"I need you—now and forever." His hold tightened, reassuring her that if he could help it she would never feel lonely again.

She sighed and rested her head in the warm hollow of his shoulder. "Luke, do you suppose we'll always fight?"

"Probably," he murmured into her hair. "But for people with our temperaments, learning how to fight is just as important as learning how to love."

"Do you think we could count this afternoon, with my shoes and your tie, as our first lesson?" she asked hopefully.

"I suppose." His chuckle reverberated in her ear. "I can hardly wait to get busy on my homework tonight."

Bonnie smiled and relaxed as he enfolded her more lovingly against his hard frame. In one way, they were back where they'd started. In another, they were light years ahead. Both of them had taken a long and painful route home, but she knew now that it was a circle with a purpose.

"I almost forgot!" She broke away and grabbed his hand. "I'm supposed to bring you home to say good-bye to Darlene and Dave. And you still have to give them the new chairs you made for them."

"One more kiss," he insisted, pulling her back into his strong arms, "and then we'll leave."

She laughed. "I think I'm hearing a seven-year-old echo."

"It worked once," he growled playfully before claiming her softly parted lips. "What's to keep it from working a second time?"

"Nothing," she whispered, kissing him twice for good measure.

It was time to go home. They linked arms and left the circle, walking side by side. Halfway across the meadow, a thistle stabbed the tender sole of her bare foot, and she yelped in pain.

He dropped to his knee and ran his thumb over the sore spot. She winced, then sighed in relief on hearing it was nothing more serious than ruined hose.

"Where are your shoes?" he demanded with a sigh of exasperation.

"Right where you threw them," she said sweetly.

They looked at each other and their laughter sounded in the twilight. Luke stood and scooped her into his arms. "What am I going to do with you, ma?"

Bonnie gazed into his twinkling eyes. "Are you open for suggestions, pa?"

They debated their options all the way home. Later, when they were finally alone, they settled the argument. On love's own terms.

Silhouette Desire

Six new titles are published on the first Friday every month. All are available at your local bookshop or newsagent, so make sure of obtaining your copies by taking note of the following dates:

NOVEMBER 2nd

NOVEMBER 30th

JANUARY 4th

FEBRUARY 1st

MARCH 1st

APRIL 5th

Silhouette Desire

Coming Next Month

Love And Old Lace by Nicole Monet

Burned once, Virginia had decided to swear off
romance and settle for a sensible, chaste
existence—but seductive Lucas Freeman
stormed her defences and neither her
body nor her heart could resist.

Wilderness Passion by Lindsay McKenna

Libby wanted to be ready for anything when she
met her unwilling partner on the environmental
expedition. But nothing prepared her for
Don Wagner, and the mountain trek suddenly
became a journey into a world of desire.

Table For Two by Josephine Charlton

Hadley and Lucas had shared a youthful love.
Now, when Hadley had landed in his embrace
once more, history repeated itself and left
them both determined that this time they
would not have to say goodbye.

Silhouette Desire

Coming Next Month

The Fires Within by Aimee Martel

As a female firefighter, Isabel was determined to be "one of the boys"—but no one made her feel more a woman than Lt. Mark Grady. Passion blazed between them, but could they be lovers *and* co-workers?

Tide's End by Erin Ross

Chemical engineer on an offshore oil rig, Holly had vowed never to engage in a "platform romance". Kirk's touch could make her forget her promises, but would his dangerous job as a diver keep them apart?

Lady Be Bad by Elaine Raco Chase

Though Noah had broken her heart six years before, Mariayna still loved him. Now she would attend his wedding with only one aim in mind—she would break all the rules to have him back again.

THE MORE SENSUAL
PROVOCATIVE ROMANCE

95p each

115 ☐ GAMBLER'S
WOMAN
Stephanie James

116 ☐ CONTROLLING
INTEREST
Janet Joyce

117 ☐ THIS BRIEF
INTERLUDE
Nora Powers

118 ☐ OUT OF
BOUNDS
Angel Milan

119 ☐ NIGHT WITH
A STRANGER
Nancy John

120 ☐ RECAPTURE
THE LOVE
Rita Clay

121 ☐ LATE RISING
MOON
Dixie Browning

122 ☐ WITHOUT
REGRETS
Brenda Trent

123 ☐ GYPSY
ENCHANTMENT
Laurie Paige

124 ☐ COLOUR MY
DREAMS
Edith St. George

125 ☐ PASSIONATE
AWAKENING
Gina Caimi

126 ☐ LEAVE ME
NEVER
Suzanne Carey

127 ☐ FABULOUS
BEAST
Stephanie James

128 ☐ POLITICAL
PASSIONS
Suzanne Michelle

129 ☐ MADISON
AVENUE
MARRIAGE
Cassandra Bishop

130 ☐ BETWEEN THE
COVERS
Laurien Blair

131 ☐ TO TOUCH
THE FIRE
Shirley Larson

132 ☐ ON LOVE'S
OWN TERMS
Cathlyn McCoy

All these books are available at your local bookshop or newsagent, or can be ordered direct from the publisher. Just tick the titles you want and fill in the form below.
Prices and availability subject to change without notice.

SILHOUETTE BOOKS, P.O. Box 11, Falmouth, Cornwall.

Please send cheque or postal order, and allow the following for postage and packing:

U.K. – 50p for one book, plus 20p for the second book, and 14p for each additional book ordered up to a £1.63 maximum.

B.F.P.O. and EIRE – 50p for the first book, plus 20p for the second book, and 14p per copy for the next 7 books, 8p per book thereafter.

OTHER OVERSEAS CUSTOMERS – 75p for the first book, plus 21p per copy for each additional book.

Name ....

Address ....

....